FIRES BENEATH THE SEA

a novel

LYDIA MILLET

Big Mouth House

Easthampton, MA

Big Mouth House
150 Pleasant Street #306
Easthampton, MA 01027
www.bigmouthhouse.net
info@bigmouthhouse.net

Distributed to the trade by Consortium.

First Edition
June 2011

Library of Congress Control Number: 2011921997

ISBN: 978-1-931520-71-3 (trade cloth); 978-1-931520-41-6 (ebook)

Text set in Minion Pro.
Printed on 50# Natures Natural 30% PCR Recycled Paper by C-M Books in Ann Arbor, MI.

For Mr. Harris

One

The end of August, after the summer people left, was Cara's favorite time of year. It was still warm enough on the Outer Cape to go to the beach and run headlong into the crashing waves. And since all the cars were gone, with their blaring horns and the smog from their tailpipes, she could ride her bike along Route 6 without feeling nervous.

After two months of crowds and backed-up traffic, the loneliness of it felt like a deep sigh of relief.

Now she was riding along the top of the tall, crumbling cliffs that overlooked the long stretch of sand and blue water that was the national seashore. The wind sighed as it ruffled the wild grass and the low, scrubby pine trees. From here, though she was high above the ocean, she could still smell the salt spray and hear the faint crash of the surf. She could even make out the small figures of people below—a few end-of-summer stragglers leading their bounding dogs along the lacy white line of the tide.

Sometimes there were ships like tiny dots in the gray haze of the distant water; sometimes there was nothing there at all. Then she could imagine she was looking all the way over the end of the earth.

If the earth had an end.

Panting, she pedaled hard along the cliff trail. She was headed to Nauset Light Beach, wearing some flips and a tank top, to meet her friend Hayley; a mesh bag was stuffed into one of the bike's saddlebags and held her swimsuit and a towel. The sand was fine and loose up here and it was hard to ride, but then, finally, the trail on the cliff's edge turned inland for a few hundred yards and emptied into the beach parking lot.

She was struggling to catch her breath when she got off and locked her bike to an old split-rail fence. Because it was late summer, and also late afternoon, the parking lot was nearly empty of cars—just a rainbow-colored hippie van in one corner and a park ranger's jeep in another. The red-and-white striped Nauset lighthouse loomed over the lake of pavement.

All the tourons, as her older brother Max and his friends called the tourists when they were acting cooler-than-thou, liked to stand in the parking lot to take pictures of the lighthouse. It was famous because it was near where telegraphs had been invented, or at least where the famous Marconi, who had the next beach over named after him, sent the first one across the Atlantic.

Telegraphs had clearly been more of a hassle than email, she thought, but like everything back then, cool in their own way.

The Park Service had a display on Marconi but she wasn't that interested. Her dad had told her Marconi stole his ideas from better men like Nikola Tesla, then took all the credit himself, and anyway Marconi was a fascist-type dude. Which wasn't too ideal.

But apparently didn't stop them from naming beaches.

"Hey, you."

Hayley was leaning against the fence along the boardwalk. She'd lived just down the street from them ever since Cara could remember, and though she and Cara were really different they'd always been best friends. Her blond hair had tiny braids at the sides, tied with elastics whose pink matched her lip gloss and bubble gum; Hayley was addicted to lip gloss and to gum.

Cara's dad, who called gum "that filthy habit" as if it were a new designer drug or something, had recently said Hayley was "like a gawky calf chewing her cud."

"What took you so long?" went on Hayley. "I've been here for ages."

"I had to help my dad with something," said Cara.

The truth was she'd been crying a bit pathetically in her room. And even though she trusted Hayley, she didn't want to overshare.

They went into the shower room to slip into their suits, Hayley's a hot-pink bikini, Cara's a one-piece blue Speedo she used for swim team. Hayley was on the team too, but when it came to beach apparel one-pieces were a fashion don't, she told Cara.

They came out of the changing room to find a big gray cloud covering the sun.

"Oh. Nice," said Hayley, shivering, and hung her towel around her neck as they headed down the wooden steps to the beach.

There were a couple of guys playing Frisbee on the sand, and an older lady reading a book, but that was it. No life-guard on duty, and the waves weren't big enough for surfers.

They laid down their towels and tested the edge of the water with their toes.

"It's freezing," groaned Hayley. "You gotta be kidding me! Like, forget it."

The ocean-side water was always colder—your lips turned blue and you started to shiver as soon as you went in. Because the Cape was a peninsula, with one side facing out to the ocean and the other facing the Massachusetts coast, the beaches on the two sides were different. The bay side, as they called the side facing in, had warmer water, which was why they usually swam either there or in the turquoise kettle ponds that dotted the piney woods. But the bayside water was often silty, too, and full of floating debris, while the ocean-side water was clear. The ocean side also had softer, whiter sand, bigger waves, and the tall, amazing bluffs.

"I'm going in anyway," said Cara. "Come on. Don't be a wuss. What if I drown because I had no swim buddy?"

"That's like emotional blackmail," said Hayley. "I think."

"Call it what you want," said Cara. "Are you a man or a mouse?"

"Mouse, chick," said Hayley. "And Miss Mousy has a magazine. But hey, you go crazy."

She backed up and settled down on her towel, and Cara waded in and stood in a foot of frigid water looking out at the rest of the ocean. She watched the sand beneath her feet get sucked out by the tide, felt her heels sink into the hollows. After a while she splashed out farther and then dove.

As the water closed over her she thought of swimming with her mother, who always dove right into the ocean, no matter how cold it was.

Her mother. Who was gone.

It was her mother who had taught her to trust the water; now the slow pull of the tide and the water's buoyancy helped her forget her worries a bit. She dove in and splashed out again, floated on her back and gazed up at the sky.

Last summer it had mostly been her two brothers and her at the beach, but this summer things had changed. Since Max was sixteen he could work at restaurants, so he'd been bussing tables during the high season, and even this week—though the crowds had thinned out and tips were nothing much once the stream of tourists slowed to a trickle—he was still working the dinner shift, which began in the late afternoons. It sounded like fun, in a way—all the wait staff and kitchen staff knew each other pretty well by the end of the season and now were a kind of big, squabbling family—but if Cara wanted to do restaurant work herself she still had three years to go.

Jax, short for Jackson, had just turned ten and was off at summer camp on the wildlife sanctuary on the bay, where the counselors filled the days dragging the kids around on what they cheerfully called "nature discovery walks" and "tidal flat funhikes." He loved spending his time outdoors and lugged home backpacks full of the big, dark-brown shells of horse-shoe crabs and slimy pieces of seaweed. He set them up on a shelf over his bed till her dad noticed the smell.

Jax had always been obsessed with animals, including extinct ones like dinosaurs and trilobites; he had spent a lot of time learning about them with their mother, who was a marine biologist. Memorizing large numbers of facts about obscure subjects was her little brother's idea of fun. Jax collected information in databases that would have been impressive for a college student, much less a kid. He was a combination of techie and nature boy, though his nature-loving was pretty scientific—more anthropology than wild child or granola. He took it upon himself to carefully record the curious habits of the natives.

But since their mother had disappeared—the 20th of June, a date they'd never forget—Jax expressed his animal interest mostly by collecting live ones in his room and for-getting they were there until it was too late. Acting out, was what Max called it. Hermit crabs, frogs, once even a foot-long dead, rotting fish with skin and meat still hanging off the bones—all kinds of things were appearing in his room that shouldn't be there. And not always in tanks or cages, either.

Her parents had adopted Jax when he was two, and by last summer her dad used to say he was nine going on ninety. Jax was different, to say the least. Sure, he was "gifted" and all that, and sometimes talked like a tenured professor—a miniature version of their dad—but it went way further than that.

Jax had certain…abilities.

She shook her head. She didn't want to think about that right now.

School was starting in a week or so, which was cool but was also making her feel anxious. She missed her mother even more because of it—her mother who always found the time to help her buy supplies and plan for extracurriculars. This year there would only be her dad, and he was almost as busy as he was absentminded. He taught history at 4C's, Cape Cod Community College, and was getting ready to start back for the fall semester, doing classes in European church history—"madmen, monks, and martyrs," as he called it fondly.

He said her mother was bound to be back any day now, and Max said so, too, but Cara knew they were saying that to make her feel better. And maybe themselves too.

She realized she was blinking up at the sky. There were more gray clouds gathering, and it was getting late.

On her way back to shore, just beyond the break, she dove under again and swam underwater for one long kick, holding her breath. Right when she was about to come up for air something brushed up against her and she practically leapt out of the water. It was something with fur. What the—?

She splashed, looking around her frantically. And there it was—something brown in the water. A small, tan-and-brown head with dark, shining eyes.

It definitely wasn't a seal—Cara had seen them plenty of times in the water from Falmouth all the way up to P-town. There were no sea lions around here, and it wasn't one of those anyway. Maybe some kind of large rodent?

Then it flipped onto its back and floated, like it was just lounging there, paws up on its belly right beneath the chin. Its eyes seemed to be steadily focused on her. And then she recognized what it was. Not from real life, only from nature shows.

It was an otter.

But she'd never heard of otters on the Cape. Never.

She treaded water, threads of seaweed clinging to her ankles…what struck her was that the otter didn't seem to be afraid of her at all. The eyes were so dark…it lay on its back and the eyes, she could swear, were like a person's: they were intently fixed on her own. Beady because they had purpose, but also soft and deep.

She'd never been so close to a wild animal. It didn't make sense; the otter should already be long gone.

"How come you aren't afraid of me?" she whispered.

It was stupid to talk to an otter, but she didn't know what else to try. The fur was beautiful, the face so light it was almost white, with a dark triangle of nose, and the paws a dark brown. She wanted to touch those handlike paws, posed thoughtfully together almost as if the otter was thinking. She could reach out easily; it was so near.

She treaded water a bit closer, a bit closer—their eyes were still locked together, it seemed to her—and then her cold, pruney fingertips were reaching out, almost without her planning it. For just a second they touched the rough black pad of a paw.

In that second it was like someone had shuffled the world away—all of it forgotten except for the feeling she was having. It was as if the sky and sea disappeared, the beach and the cliffs faded. She felt dizzy and almost sick but also curiously warm.

She felt exhilarated.

And then it streamed through her:

TAKE CARE OF THEM FOR ME TAKE CARE OF THEM FOR ME TAKE CARE OF THEM

"*Cara!* Hey Cara! You coming out any time soon?"

It was Hayley, calling from shore. She sounded so far away, though. Cara's eyes were open again, the sea was there, the beach, the different blues and browns of normal life, the scene of ocean and sky. She found herself shaking her head—had those been her own thoughts?

But it didn't feel like it; it didn't feel like she'd *chosen* to think those things, and the words left a trail behind them in her mood, a kind of glittering hope…and then the otter was flipping over so quickly she couldn't follow the movement, and it was gone.

She stared at where it had been. Nothing but water.

She shook her head, dazed. She felt a bizarre glow, like a line of silver through the middle of her body.

It lingered.

Finally, not knowing what else to do, she swam slowly for the beach, then waded out and ran, tossing up sand, to where Hayley was lying on her towel flipping magazine pages.

"Did you see that?" she asked, breathless. "Did you see what was right next to me?"

"You're totally dripping, Car! And there's sand on my back now!"

"Sorry, but didn't you—"

"Wait. Wait. Listen. *Accessorize for fall with shades of oxblood and burgundy,*" read Hayley. "There's an actual color called oxblood? Barfo. Hey. What's the difference between lime and chartreuse?"

"But—there was an animal! An otter! I swear, Hay. Can you believe that?"

"Otters. Uh-huh."

Hayley nodded distractedly and turned her magazine to look at something from a different angle. It seemed to be a picture of a model's thin wrist wearing 8,000 bangles.

Cara couldn't pay attention to anything but that silver trace she still felt in herself, her whole being that tingled with the fleeting touch of something unknown.

"Hayley, listen. Do you realize how weird that is? We don't have otters in the ocean here. At least, I've never heard of one."

"Maybe the little guy got lost," mused Hayley and looked up. "But they can swim, right? Is there an otter-rescue deal, like there is for beached whales?"

Cara stared at her for a second, then sighed and settled down on her own towel. Sometimes Hay could be a little clueless.

But sea otters, Cara was almost certain, lived on the West Coast. In the Pacific. Not in the Atlantic at all. It was really kind of impossible. She made a mental note to ask Jax about it. Jax or her dad.

And then, on top of that, it was as though it had talked to her without opening its mouth—as though, let's face it, it was *delivering a message*.

She lay there for a minute, tuning out completely while Hayley chattered on about some movie star who'd had an operation to make her lips fat. After a while she turned on her side and slipped her cell out of her bag to glance at its clock. It was already time to go; she had to get home for dinner.

"Man. I wish I could take off too, but I have to wait for my mom," said Hayley apologetically. "Otherwise I'd totally go with you. Sorry. She's coming after work, she's all, 'I have to get in my tan time!' Even though it'll be, like, five-thirty. It's so humiliating, she has one of those retro silver screens from the eighties? And she holds it under her chin to get more sun on her face? I go, 'Haven't you ever heard of skin cancer? Gross gnarly skin wrinkles?' I'm serious, she's gonna look like one of those orange Florida ladies."

"My mom's the opposite," said Cara. "She always makes us wear sunscreen. Even when it's gray out…"

She trailed off. Because clearly her mother wasn't around to give advice.

Hayley shot her a look, then said, more gently than usual, "Is there—do they have any, like, new info? About what might have happened?"

Cara shook her head, her eyes downcast.

There was a lump in her throat.

And a good possibility, she added to herself, that she was experiencing some kind of hallucinations.

After a minute Hayley filled the silence.

"Yeah. Well. My mom just doesn't get it. When I tell her she's getting a rhino hide she just goes, 'You have to suffer to be beautiful, Hayley.'"

Cara nodded and tried on a quick, tight smile.

Hayley reached over and grabbed her hand, squeezing it. After a few seconds, Cara moved her hand away, blinking.

"So anyway," said Hayley. "Sorry I can't ride home with you."

"No problem," said Cara and waved as she turned to head up the cliff staircase. "See you."

Tonight her dad had promised to take them to the Wellfleet Drive-In, the only drive-in movie theater left on the Cape. It was a ten-minute car ride from their rambling old house on the bay, but they were planning to take their bikes instead;

they didn't need the car, since they would probably see one of the indoor movies in the multiplex part of the drive-in. After the movie, in the dark, they would coast home again along the peaceful streets, listening to the crickets. They did it every Thursday night in the summer.

Their dad was a distracted scholar type who knew Latin and wore three-piece suits and even the kind of watch you kept in a pocket on your vest and pulled out on a chain called a fob. But he did love one modern thing: movies. He would see anything that was playing, but he especially loved bad vintage movies with cheesy special effects, like *The Mummy's Hand* and *Swamp Thing*.

She didn't know what was at the theater tonight, but this was one time she agreed with her dad: any old movie would do. When she settled down in front of the vast screen, bright pictures flashing in front of her eyes in the dark, she could almost forget that her mother was missing and no one in the whole world seemed to have the faintest clue where she was.

She walked through the wild beach roses to the parking lot. The pink flowers had already disappeared from their low bushes along the trails, leaving the rose hips behind them. Her mother liked to gather the small fruits every fall and make tea with them, which she said helped to ward off colds. At the thought, Cara felt the usual pang.

This fall, maybe, she'd get sicker than usual. This fall there wouldn't be the warm homemade tea, only the bare counter in the kitchen and empty oven mitts hanging on hooks, unused.

She looked up at the sky, to where the towering white clouds of the morning had flattened out and turned gray and low, and tried to push the thought of winter down and away. Unlocking her bike, she tossed her mesh bag into a saddlebag, got on and took off. With no one in the parking lot except her, she could fly; she could pedal as fast as she wanted across the pavement, through the cooling air of twilight.

She spread out her arms and felt the wind lift her hair.

⚼

As she coasted down her street toward her house the surface of the bayside water was turning black; fingers of pink and purple reached across the sky. The trees were shifting slowly from leafy green into dark silhouettes, making home seem even more welcoming.

Her family's house was big and ramshackle on the outside but cozy within: the warm orange light from the windows reflected across the water and shone through the trees. It was built of weathered silver-gray wood and had started out as a simple box, long ago, but more and more additions had been built onto it over the years. Now it had a wraparound, covered porch overlooking the water on one side and the grassy lawn on the other, where she and Max played badminton and Jax jumped in between them, trying to bat the birdie out of the air with his grubby hand.

During the day, if you sat on the bayside terrace, you could watch boats chugging out to the oyster fields. The harbor was narrow here, and right across from her house she could see the pier with its outdoor restaurant, a fish place that always had long lines in the summer. At night the restaurant sparkled with light, and the sounds of people laughing carried over the water.

She lifted her bike up the sagging wooden steps and leaned it beside the front door, near the pile of her dad's sea kayaks. Her dad wasn't the sporty type—that was an under-statement, actually—but he liked paddling, as he called it, and used to make the family do it, all together on the weekends.

Not recently.

As soon as she banged through the screen door into the front hall, she smelled cooking. She hung her bag on a peg, kicked off her shoes, and shoved them into a jumble of hightops and sneakers piled up against the wall. The house wasn't so neat these days. She heard the thump of music above her head, from Max's room. Max was really into old classics—mostly the Clash, at the moment. Since their mother had gone, he liked to shut himself up a lot and blast it really loud.

Jax was more interested in dead toads.

Rufus, their aging brown Lab, came up to her wagging his tail. She knelt down and petted his head.

"I'm home," she called out to her dad, rising and making her way down the hall to the kitchen. Rufus followed, his nails clicking on the wood floor.

But when she reached the kitchen door, a woman she'd never seen before was standing at the stove.

"Who are *you*?" she blurted.

The woman turned. She had a broad front, a sun-weathered face, and graying hair pulled back in a pony-tail. She wore a red-and-white checked apron that said IF YOU DON'T LIKE MY COOKING...LOWER YOUR STANDARDS.

"You must be Cara!" she said and wiped her hands on her apron so she could stick one out. "Call me Lolly. Your father hired me to do some housekeeping. And dinners."

Seeing Cara's blank face, she added quickly: "Just, you know. Till your mother gets back and can pitch in again."

"Oh," said Cara in a small voice. "I see. Nice to meet you."

"With him starting back to teaching, and all," went on Lolly, "and you three kids at two different schools, things will be getting pretty hectic. Hey. You like mac and cheese?"

"Sure, sure," said Cara, distracted. "So, um, where *is* my dad?"

"Should be in his study."

Cara turned and left the kitchen, making her way over the thick boards of the dining room floor to her dad's half-open door.

"Cara, dear," he said when she pushed it open further, looking up over the glasses that were set low on his nose. He was reading in his armchair, legs crossed. "How was the beach?"

"You hired a *housekeeper*?" she asked.

"Apparently," said her dad.

16

"But what if—you know—I mean she could come home any day, couldn't she?"

"When your mother comes home, Lolly will go," he said gently. "She needed to pick up a few hours. She has a two-year-old grandson she takes care of. I'm sure you'll like her cooking."

Cara nodded, the tense feeling in her stomach growing a little less.

Her dad was sad, she thought. Just like her.

"Very good, then," he said, and went back to his reading. When he was reading, he was lost to the world.

Softly she walked over to the big dictionary he kept on a stand in the corner. Under the cover he'd tucked the note her mother left. She didn't know if he'd even noticed she'd found it, but she liked to go into his study when he was out and just gaze at the note, smoothing her fingers over the scrawled words her mother had written.

Now she turned the heavy sheaf of pages over and exposed the fragment.

Have to go. Danger. Keep them safe — love

That was all.

Now, with her hand touching the worn paper, she felt tears filling her eyes. It had been two months, and there was still no sign of her mother coming back. No one was doing anything to help, either. The police hadn't taken it seriously. Despite her mother's note—the word *danger* echoed in Cara's head when she was trying to fall asleep—the cops obviously thought her mother had left her dad. For some other guy.

They had looked at the pictures of her mother in the family albums—her mother was beautiful, with long dark hair, olive skin, and green eyes, and people often thought she was Cara's sister—and then looked at her dad, in his glasses and vest, and decided it was a "routine domestic situation." Cara had heard one of them say that when they didn't think any kids were listening.

She'd felt so bad for her dad. It was like the cops didn't think he was good enough for her mother.

But he was. They all were. They were all good enough for each other.

It wasn't like that.

"Sweetheart," came her dad's gruff voice behind her, as he put a hand on her shoulder, "don't worry. Your mother is a strong person. She can take care of herself. And she *will* come back to us."

She wiped away the tear that had leaked out, sniffed, and turned around.

"OK," she said stiffly, and gave a small nod. If she hugged him she would lose it.

Standing there together, they heard the low roll of thunder.

"Well, I guess we'll be driving to the movies after all," said her dad.

She trudged up the creaky staircase to take a shower before dinner. Max's door, at the end of the hall, had a glossy picture of Joe Strummer on it. Jax's, on the other end of the hall beside her own door, featured your typical Einstein-with-messy-hair photo. It was taped right on top of an older poster of fossils.

She didn't know if Jax was a genius Einstein-style, exactly, but he definitely had some kind of photographic memory—among other things. Last year his elementary school had wanted him to skip three years, which would have put him in Cara's grade at Nauset. Luckily her parents had said no, because even if he was a brainiac he was still just a ten-year-old at heart. Since June 20th he had been teaching himself about Great Geniuses of the Past: Mozart, Shakespeare, Marie Curie, Kurt Gödel, and sometimes child prodigies like Bobby Fischer.

It hadn't escaped Cara's notice that a lot of the Great Geniuses of the Past hadn't ended up too happy.

She knocked sharply on Einstein's face.

"Enter please," said Jax, using his most annoying robot voice.

She pushed the door open. The room smelled like a moldy sock.

"Ew," she said, wrinkling her nose.

Jax was sitting on the floor, books spread open around him, fooling with a database on his laptop.

"Did you meet the housekeeper?" she asked.

Jax nodded, intent on his database.

"So? What did you think?"

She always asked what Jax thought of new people. Jax had a way of knowing things he shouldn't know, and if he didn't trust someone, she'd learned from experience to steer clear of them herself. One guy who mowed their lawn last year had gotten Jax's thumbs-down even though he seemed really friendly; then it turned out he was some kind of perv. A lady at the post office told them: outside the Stop & Shop, men in suits came and took him away.

Now Jax gave her a thumbs-up. Lolly must be OK.

Cara leaned in close to see what he was typing about.

"Watch out. Right foot," he said, never looking away from the screen, and kept typing rapidly on the keyboard.

She glanced down and narrowly missed stepping on a big snail that had left a slimy trail on his floor.

"Jax!" she said, irritated. "You're not supposed to do that!"

"There is a prejudice in this house against gastropod mollusks," said Jax sternly.

He used even bigger words than her dad, the PhD. It was one reason most kids his age made fun of him and the only real friend he had was a bigger geek than he was. She was glad he was past his "citations phase," at least. That was what her parents had called it. The citations phase was when he used to give footnotes for practically everything he said, like "*Scientific American*, September 1997, Volume 277 #3, pages 70-75."

It had been pretty tough to talk to him during the citations. Her parents had made him get checked for Asperger syndrome, but it turned out he didn't have it.

"Uh-huh," she said.

"And also against chelicerate arthropods and decapod crustaceans."

"Talk normally," said Cara, impatient.

When her dad wanted Jax to speak so that average people like her or Max could understand him, he always said *Jackson, please use the King's English.*

"Horseshoe and hermit crabs. As you may know, neither is a true crab per se."

She sighed.

"I could have squished it."

"But you didn't."

She thought about telling him about the otter. She'd meant to when she came in. But now, somehow, she felt like letting it slide.

Because that was the other thing about Jax, the other thing that made him different from everyone else she knew. If he wanted to, Jax could suss out what she was thinking without asking her.

Jax, basically, had some form of ESP.

He didn't like it when she called it that. He said there was nothing extrasensory about it, that it wasn't paranormal but as scientific as anything else—just not yet understood.

Whatever it was, it made her hemmed in and claustrophobic: when Jax felt like reading her, her brain had no privacy. She'd seen him do it with Max occasionally, and even their dad—know what they thought before they said it, anyway—but the other guys didn't seem to notice. Or if they did, at least, they didn't say anything.

She'd told him not to do it with her, that it wasn't his business what she was thinking unless she wanted to tell him. But sometimes she suspected he was doing it anyway. And one time, recently, he'd spied on her for sure—about a guy she liked, though only for about three seconds—and it was so embarrassing it had made her feel sick to her stomach.

He called it *pinging*. He *pinged* people.

Anyway, if he really wanted to know about the otter, she figured, he probably already would.

"I'm taking a shower," she said, "so don't flush the toilet," and she went out and closed his door behind her.

Their house had eccentric plumbing; sometimes the shower water turned scalding hot if someone turned on the cold water in another room.

It was only while she was standing under the shower nozzle, feeling the warm water fall on her face, that it occurred to her: Jax and the otter—the otter who had spoken into her mind—might have more than a little bit in common.

❦

"Pleash pash the rollsh," said Max over dinner, his mouth so full of corn on the cob that Cara could barely understand him.

They were all sitting in the dining room, at the same oval wooden table they'd always sat at for dinner, with the same striped cotton napkins and polished wooden napkin rings. Above them was a dusty chandelier, and alongside the wall was a wooden sideboard beneath a large painting of the ocean with soaring white birds.

They'd taken one of the chairs away from the table a few weeks ago so they didn't have to look at it, standing there empty, while they ate.

Max—still talking with his mouth full about something she couldn't quite make out—was pretty much the opposite of Jax: girls loved him, and, being good at running and basketball, he was popular with boys too. He was smart enough, but he put his energy into other things, so he barely squeaked by at school. This summer he'd been using his money from the restaurant job to buy boards and board stuff, and hanging out a lot at the skatepark. And it was even harder than usual to get his attention. When he wasn't at the restaurant, the park, or in his bedroom with the stereo volume turned way up, he was plugged into his iPod.

She had to admit, Lolly was a way better cook than their dad, whose range was limited to soup from a can and frozen pizzas that he took out of the oven when they were still cold in the middle. Tonight they were having baked macaroni, roasted corn on the cob, fresh rolls, salad, and for dessert a homemade strawberry rhubarb pie cooling on the sideboard.

"So," said their dad, holding a newspaper open, "we may have to rush when we're finished eating. Playing at the right time: a cartoon, an historical epic that involves cutlasses and ships, and a thriller that's probably too scary for Jax."

"I want to see the thriller that's probably too scary for Jax," said Jax.

"R rating," said their dad.

"The cutlashes," said Max, still chewing.

"The ships," agreed Cara.

"The cutlasses used in films," intoned Jax, "are often his-torically inaccurate, nineteenth-century weapons."

"That is correct, Jackson," said their dad.

Just then rain started beating down on the roof. Cara loved that pattering sound.

"Everyone's bedroom windows closed?" asked their dad.

But the next moment Jax was staring into the front hall. Cara followed his gaze and saw only the closed screen door and the dimness of the unlit porch beyond.

"Jax?" asked Max.

Jax didn't break his stare. Rufus, lying on the floor beside him with his chin on his paws, stood up and looked in the same direction, his tail held low.

"Jax," urged Cara. "What is it?"

Slowly, still not blinking or looking at them, Jax raised one hand and pointed at the front door.

Their dad scraped his own chair back and walked to the door; Cara watched as he pushed it open.

"Hello?" he called, into the dark. "Anyone there?"

They waited silently. Cara's stomach flipped. What if— what if…could it be *her?*

Jax's finger still hovered in the air, pointing.

Their dad flicked on the outside light. The rain picked up.

"No one," he said breezily, closing the outside door behind him. He sat down at his place again.

"What *was* that, Jax?" asked Cara. "Huh? Did you see something?"

Jax finally dropped his finger. After a moment he shrugged and shook his head, smiling at Lolly, who'd come in to cut the pie.

"He was playing with us," said Max under his breath. "He's just looking for attention."

That made Cara feel bad for Jax. He was never nasty on purpose.

Still, she felt a hole in the pit of her stomach. He'd gotten her hopes up, even if he didn't mean to.

In some ways he was still a baby, boy telepath or not. Before their mother left, he still slept in their parents' bed when he got scared at night. Now he crept into her own room sometimes, because he had nowhere else to go. Their dad had taken to working late most nights since their mother had left and usually fell asleep on the couch in his study, his desk light still on, a thin blanket hastily pulled over his legs. So Jax couldn't curl up with him.

"OK, moviegoers," said her dad, and laid down his napkin. "We have six minutes for pie-eating. Then on to swashbuckling. No disrespect to your baking skills, Lolly, but eat fast, kids."

"Underappreciated," said Lolly. "That's my lot in life."

❦

By the time they drove home from the movie, it was raining hard, and trees were whipping around in the wind. They'd all raced to the car from the shelter of the theater lobby but got drenched anyway, and now Cara and Jax sat shivering in the back with a fleece blanket pulled over them. The wipers made a rapid *thwock, thwock* across the cracked windshield of their beat-up wagon as Max and their dad, in the front, argued about the star of the movie.

"You've gotta be kidding," said Max. "He was supposed to be what—a French naval officer? He sounded like he was from New Jersey."

"I didn't think the accent was so New Jersey," said her dad. "Maybe Normandy coast. The peasantry, of course."

"Get out," said Max, and cuffed him on the shoulder.

Then he put his iPod buds in his ears, sank down in the passenger seat, and turned to gaze out the window, beating the rhythm of his music on the seat cushion with one hand.

"Gimme that," said Cara to Jax. "Hey! You stole, like, the whole blanket."

Jax said nothing, only shivered, so she let it go. Water coursed down the glass, and for the hundredth time she ran through the brief words of the note in her head. *Have to go. Danger.* What could it mean? Her mother didn't exactly live on the edge; she was a biologist, after all, not a James Bond type. She worked at the far end of the Cape, at Woods Hole Oceanographic Institution, where she studied seals and other marine mammals. Her mother was beautiful and generous and everyone loved her. What danger could there possibly be?

Cara felt a flush of fear.

She's totally OK, she thought. She's fine.

But if she was fine, why wasn't she back by now?

Their dad spun the wheel, and they turned and headed up their own street, which sloped toward the water's edge. Suddenly their headlights swept over something out of place, and she stared out her window as they passed.

It was a tall, blurred figure, hooded. Maybe wearing a dark coat or a cape; she thought it must be a man, from the size, but she couldn't see the face.

The figure was just standing there, facing them, arms hanging down at his sides. He didn't move a muscle. In the night, in the rain.

But stranger than that, the strangest part of all, was that it looked like he was *floating in water*.

It looked like he was surrounded by it—not by raindrops but by solid water, suspended in it. Hanging.

She felt the tiny hairs on her arms prickle.

"Jax! Did you see that guy?"

Jax, teeth chattering, swiveled to look out the rear window.

"A person in a hood or something, just standing stock-still in—in the rain," she said. "Did you see him?"

Jax turned back to face forward, his eyes glazed over and slightly dull.

"That wasn't a person," he said.

A few minutes later she tucked him in, as she often did after he finished reading (at the moment it was *A Brief History of Time*). She pulled the curtains and checked the floor for snails, frogs, and lizards. One disgusting experience involving her bare feet and a cicada had made her extra careful.

"They're all in the tanks," said Jax sleepily, rubbing his eyes.

She turned out every light but his favorite lamp, a scale model of the moon. Impact craters and all.

"So Jax," she said as she sat down on the bed and pulled the blanket up to his chin, "what did you mean, that wasn't a person? You kind of creeped me out tonight."

Jax turned over, his eyelids heavy.

"He was the one who came to dinner. The one who was at our front door," he murmured.

She felt a chill come over her.

"So...," she said slowly, "what did you mean by *not a person*?"

"He didn't have a signal," Jax said, and burrowed into his pillow.

He'd tried to explain to her once, the time when she got mad at him for pinging her, that pinging was like reading the patterns of energy in people's brains—not the kind of passive, low-level sensing he did when he first met people and decided whether he could trust them, but a more intense kind of interpreting. A kind of decoding. Jax wasn't proud of himself when he pinged, but sometimes he couldn't resist.

He called the energy patterns he sensed a "signal," even though that wasn't technically what it was, he said.

"Maybe you just couldn't read him," she suggested.

"Nothing to read," he mumbled. "He was just…"

He turned onto his other side, his eyes closing.

"…not alive."

And then he fell asleep.

Two

Cara woke up as dawn was breaking, a faint light leaking through her window blinds. To her the morning felt quiet and almost disappointed, the way it always did after a big rain, with the slow *drip-drip-drip* of water off branches and leaves.

She crossed the cool bedroom floor in her bare feet. Her room was at the back of the house, on the bay side, which meant she had a view—over the porch roof that sloped down beneath her window, through some feathery branches—of the water and the sky across Cape Cod Bay. If you flew straight inland, her mother had once told her, you would see Plymouth Rock and the fake Mayflower ship they kept moored there for tourons.

Max's room faced south and Jax's north; her parents used to sleep in the big single room of the attic, right under the sloped roof, with a big glass skylight overhead. Her mother liked to lie in bed and look up at the stars.

She walked lightly down the stairs. Rufus was curled up on the runner in the front hall; he'd kept a vigil there every night since her mother had disappeared.

"Come on, Roof," she said. She snapped on his leash and slipped into her flip-flops.

They walked along the pretty residential streets bordering the marshes till they got to a lonely sand road that wound past a small, reedy shellfish cove. The ground was covered with tiny fiddler crabs that skittered into their holes in great waves. She and her mother used to walk Rufus here together; her mother had pointed out those tiny crabs, as well as the big osprey nests on their manmade posts rising out of the wetlands.

There was no one around, and the sand was wet from the rain. She listened to the *crunch, crunch, crunch* of her sneakers across its grainy surface.

"OK, Rufus," she said finally, and unclipped the leash. At the end of the road, sticking up on the other side of a dune, was a modern-looking beach house that was all glass and sharp angles. It was a rental property, and outside the high season it was mostly empty. "Run!"

In the cool of the morning she watched him go—farther and farther away, till he rounded the bend of the dune and was lost to view.

Then she started walking after him, her mind wandering. Her dad had said hurricanes to the south were bringing the storms, and this was hurricane season. He said the hurricanes were getting bigger these days than they used to be, growing more powerful and coming more often.

She felt a shiver of foreboding.

"Rufus!" she called.

The sun slanted off the roof of the big modern house as she shaded her eyes to squint at it. Maybe, she thought, he'd found something at the waterline, a fish to gnaw or a crab to paw.

But then he reappeared, running. Nearer, nearer, nearer, and she saw he was wagging his tail. He looked happier than he had the whole summer. And just as she'd thought, he was carrying some kind of bone in his mouth.

"Hi again, boy," she said, and rubbed behind his ears.

Instead of worrying the bone, he dropped it in front of her. It was actually a piece of wet driftwood.

"I don't want that, Roof," she said. "I don't chew on sticks like you do. Remember?"

He nosed it toward her feet and knelt, paws together, in front of it. Tail still wagging, tongue out.

"You want me to throw it?"

She picked it up and tossed; he wheeled and fetched it.

"Let's keep walking," she said. "We can play fetch when we get home."

But he dropped it in front of her again and barked once, loudly.

"Geez, Roof," she said, and picked it up. She would have to carry it.

Then she noticed.

Lightly scratched words. The letters were so thin she could barely read them.

CONSULT THE LEATHERBACK.

She turned it over. There was one more word.

CARA.

She dropped it, shocked. Her hand was shaking.

"Who gave this to you, Rufus?" she asked the dog, leaning down and gripping his sandy snout in her hand.

He just kept wagging his tail.

Maybe it was one of her friends, messing with her head. Maybe Hayley or Jade? But Hayley didn't come up here, as far as Cara knew. Plus these days she was busy in the mornings because she went to work with her mother, who ran a hair salon. She helped out with the shampooing.

And Cara's other best friend, Jade, had gone up to Maine with her family till school started. They didn't like the crowds.

Anyway, this was way too weird for either of them.

When she and Rufus reached the end of the road, and the tide was practically lapping at her feet, she couldn't see anyone at all. Not even a fishing boat on the water. The big modern house looked locked up and empty.

Rufus gave a low *woof*, his sound of recognition.

"What now?"

And then she saw something in the waves—round, small, and brown. Dark eyes. She was astounded: it was another otter. She could hardly believe it. First the ocean side, now the bay…it was a plague of otters, practically.

She had to remember to ask Jax about it. Maybe, with global warming, otters were migrating differently these days, or something.

After all, two summers ago great white sharks had been found swimming in the waters off Chatham. That June, dozens of dead sea lions had washed up on the shore. And a couple of summers earlier, a Florida manatee had swum into the mouth of the Hudson River and then headed past the Cape, too.

None of that was supposed to happen.

And now, two sea otters. Sea otters that were supposed to live in a whole other ocean.

But there was no sign of anyone who could have given Rufus the piece of wood. All she saw was the high tide lapping at the toes of her sneaks.

When the waves pulled back they left tiny airholes in the sand.

⚓

Jax had left by the time she got home, picked up by the camp carpool, and Max and his friend Zee, short for Zadie— who wasn't his girlfriend, though Cara thought maybe she wouldn't mind—were getting ready to ride their bikes to the tennis courts before it got too hot.

"Look," she said to Max, and held out the driftwood.

He turned it over and over.

"Uh, that's great, Car. A piece of wood. Real awesome find."

She grabbed it back and studied it. It was dry now, and you couldn't really see the words anymore—they must have been etched too lightly, because all that was left was a couple of lines where the C and K had been. They looked like random chicken scratches.

"They're gone," she muttered.

"What?"

"The words. Max, someone had scratched a message on it—my name and the words *Consult the leatherback.*"

Max stopped putting his helmet on and looked at her curiously. Then he laid a hand across her forehead.

"You cool? Don't go getting spooky on me, sis," he said. "We don't need two Jaxes in the family."

"C'mon, Max," called Zee from the street. She was already on her bike, impatient. "We barely have time for a set. I gotta be at the boat by 10:30!"

"Coming," he called, and pushed off, jumping the curb. She watched them pedal away, dipping and weaving their bikes playfully under the pitch pine and bear oak trees.

She couldn't blame him. Max was the practical one in the family, even if he wasn't his usual friendly self lately; and the words definitely seemed to be gone.... She felt lonely and wanted to call Hayley, but Hayley was still working. Her mom got mad when she talked on her cell at work.

Consult the leatherback.

⊰⊱

Her dad was supposed to drive her to the Hyannis mall to buy school clothes. But she knew he'd only agreed to it to be a dutiful parent, so her heart wasn't really in it, either.

"I can just buy stuff online, if you want," she said to him in the kitchen, where he stood drinking his last cup of morning coffee. The kitchen windows faced the water, and lately her dad had a habit of just standing there staring out, his mug forgotten in his hand.

"It's Jax's last day at camp," said her dad slowly. "How about we pick him up and go on a whale watch? Teddy Soderstrom's boat has empty seats since it's the end of the season. He just called to see if we wanted to hitch a ride. It's been a while, hasn't it?"

Teddy was an old friend of the family who was also the captain of one of the whale-watch boats in Provincetown.

"OK," she said.

As they drove to Jax's camp Cara considered telling her dad about the driftwood. What if it was someone stalking her or something? *Danger.*

Then again, maybe she'd made up the words. Maybe, as Max had hinted and she herself feared, she was losing it a bit. And her dad already had enough to worry about.

"Why don't you go find your brother," said her dad when they pulled into the parking lot. "I'll wait here."

She wove through the milling crowds in the nature center lobby till she found Jax standing beneath a display on crabs, with a giant pink crab model in the middle. He was typing on his phone.

Of course, it was more than a phone. It was one of those all-you-can-eat smartphone deals: GPS, video, Internet, blah blah blah. You could point it at a star in the night sky, and it would tell you the name of the constellation.

Jax was the most teched-out family member by far. He had to be, according to him. *Data are key.*

"Hi, Cara. The European green crab, *Carcinus maenas,* is believed to consume approximately $44 million in New England shellfish per year," he said, then looked up from the phone and smiled sweetly.

"Very interesting," she said, taking his hand. "Want to go see whales?"

"*Carcinus maenas* is among the 100 worst invasive species in the world," he went on.

"I need to talk to you in private," she said, steering him out through the front doors toward the car. "Once we're on the whale boat. Dad'll probably get talking to Teddy and then come and find me. OK?"

"Sure," said Jax easily, and slid into the backseat.

"Hello, Jackson," said their dad. "Did the camping session come to a satisfactory conclusion?"

"Enh," said Jax, and shrugged. "I give it a 6.8. High marks for red-tailed hawks, eels, and square-backed marsh crabs. Low marks for food. Too much Chex Mix. Mid-range marks for so-called leadership. I like that guy Robin, he's nice, but Amy, the other counselor? Everything she says goes up at the end like a question. Even if it's not an interrogative at all. 'This is a nature experience? So I'd like you to put away all your portable electronics? That means you Jax?' Or when I was collecting specimens, she goes, 'I don't think picking that *up* is too *appropriate*?' Like that."

"Possibly insecure," said their dad, nodding sagely.

"Dim bulb," said Jax.

"So we're going to P-town to see whales," went on their dad. "Did Cara tell you? Last time we were out on a whale-watching boat, you were five. Do you remember?"

"There is ample evidence that cetaceans are stressed by whale-watching ecotourism, which can affect their behavior, migration, and breeding," said Jax.

"But you're the guy who brings baby frogs into his bedroom, then leaves them under a cushion," said Cara. "Doesn't that affect their behavior, migration, and whatever?"

"Few frog species participate in seasonal migrations," said Jax.

"Argh," said Cara.

⊰⊱

At the end of the gangplank, her dad was clapped heartily on the back by the captain, an old friend. Like his namesake stuffed bear, Teddy was big, puffy, and comforting.

"Welcome aboard, Sykes family," he boomed. "Lemme show you my latest gadgets." And he toured them around the boat, pointing out computer hardware and fancy seat covers.

He was trying to be jovial, Cara could tell, but once he leaned close to her dad and said something low. Her dad shook his head, and Teddy gripped his shoulder as though to strengthen him.

They were talking about her mother, obviously. Her parents' friends didn't like to ask about her mother being missing in front of her or Max or Jax, she'd noticed—as if, when they acted like everything was business as usual, that would keep the kids happy....

Finally the boat motored away from the pier and Cara was able to get Jax alone at the rail while their dad, who barely knew Mac from PC and claimed to believe that cell phones "might well be the Devil's handiwork," pretended to be interested in Teddy's new high-tech gadgets.

She told Jax about the driftwood message, quickly and half whispering.

"Max thinks I'm crazy," she said when she finished, and rolled her eyes, ready for Jax to make fun of her, too.

But his small face looked serious.

"Jax? What is it?"

"I don't know," he said solemnly, and shook his head. "But it has to do with her. Just like he did."

"*He?*"

"The man in the rain."

"You didn't tell me he had something to do with Mom!"

"I'm not sure," he said. "I just have a feeling."

She looked into his blue eyes and knew he believed it.

"Max would say we're both crazy," she said.

"Then don't tell him," said Jax.

"By the way," she said, remembering. "I also saw two otters. I swear! One yesterday, another one this morning. I was going to tell you before, but then I figured—actually, I was thinking about the last time you spied on me."

"I'm sorry about that," said Jax, and looked down, a bit ashamed.

"Mmm," said Cara.

"I didn't mean to, you know," he mumbled after a pause.

"I guess," said Cara.

But even if that was true—and she thought she believed him—in a way she didn't care, because the point was that whether he had meant it or not, it had still been really, really embarrassing. No one should be able to see the truly private stuff.

"Anyway," she said awkwardly. "Have you ever heard of otters around here?"

"There are still river otters in some coastal marshes," said Jax slowly, "but I wouldn't think there'd be any on the Cape."

"The first one I saw was at Nauset Light. Floating on its back."

Jax shook his head, perplexed. "But lying on their backs is a sea otter behavior. There shouldn't be any sea otters for thousands of miles!"

"That's what I thought," said Cara.

They didn't talk for a minute, staring down at the boat's white wake as it curled away behind them.

"So what do you think the message means?" she asked finally. "*Consult the leatherback* made me think of an old book or something. But it's actually a kind of big sea turtle, right?"

"I have to think about that one," said Jax.

"Look! There!" said a tourist lady. "A whale! Spouting!"

The engine throttled down as the boat came about.

"That's a pilot whale," said Teddy.

All Cara could see was a grayish hump—that was her problem with whale-watching. It was all humps that looked like rocks. Whales were cool, but you could see more of them on nature shows.

Still, it was probably better to be here than dragging around the mall while her dad asked her questions like *Why do some of the boys wear their pants so ridiculously baggy, and the others wear them so tight?*

Jax pulled out his phone and took a picture.

※

Later, lying in bed, she had a long talk on her own cell phone—basic, not smart—with Hayley, in her own bed a few doors down the street. They had a plan where the minutes were free if you waited till late enough.

She told Hayley about the driftwood.

"Are you smoking something?" asked Hayley. "First there were those ocean beavers, now this."

"Not beavers, Hay."

"Chillax. You're kind of freaking me out here."

Hayley moved on to other subjects—who would talk to them at school this fall and who would ignore them; whether her mom would give her a big enough allowance for her to "accessorize." She and her mom often struggled pretty hard with money, and Cara thought it made her feel better about it to treat it like it was trivial, like all it would affect was her fashion stylings....

After they hung up, Cara fell asleep with her reading light on. The next thing she knew, Jax was tugging at her arm. Since her mother left, he did that sometimes—came in at two or three in the morning to ask if he could sleep in her room.

"What is it, Jax?" she asked blearily, propping herself up on her elbows. "You want to sleep in here?"

Her little brother, in ancient pajamas speckled with dinosaurs, shook his head.

"You sure? It's OK if you do."

"It's not that," he whispered. "It's that he's...*here.*"

Cara sat bolt upright.

"He?"

"You know. The *guy.*"

"Here *where?*"

"Outside the door. The front door of the house."

"Should we get Dad? What should we do?"

"He doesn't want Dad. He wants us."

"But I—you said he didn't have a—a signal."

"He doesn't. But he still communicates."

She didn't want anything to do with it. It was giving her a sickening feeling.

TAKE CARE OF THEM....

Who? Jax? Max? Who else *could* it be?

"Why should we talk to him? It's night, Jax. It's scary!"

"I have to. He calls and calls, Cara. Into my head. It's like someone's yelling at me. He won't stop till we go down to him."

"It's not safe, Jax. Let's wait him out, just wait until he leaves. You can go up to Dad's room. Or stay in here tonight. With me."

She patted her coverlet.

But Jax shook his head.

"I can't. He's *blaring* at me."

Maybe Jax *is* making this up, she thought hopefully. After all, we're talking about Jax here: a pretty weird kid. Maybe this is all in his head, and if I'm supposed to take care of him, then it's my job to listen. And watch him.

"OK," she said slowly. "What do you want me to do, then?"

He turned, and she got up and followed, shutting Rufus in her room so he wouldn't bark and wake everyone.

Outside her room she flicked on the hall light, then the light over the stairs. Every light switch she saw, she flicked. Anything to make it brighter and more everyday.

Down they went, Jax padding ahead of her in his sock feet.

Their front door was old, thick with multiple coats of paint; the top half had a rectangular window with diamond-shaped panes.

"Is it locked?" she whispered.

Jax nodded.

"It's too high up for me to get a good view," he said.

So she stepped in front of him. She stood at the door and reached over to the wall, to the light switch for the porch.

She flicked it upward.

And gasped, jumping back and banging into Jax.

There he was.

The glass in the door pane made things blurry, but it was definitely him. He stood on the porch steps, facing right at them, his arms hanging at his sides. He had the same dark coat on, with the hood, but now the hood was back so she could see his face—sort of. It was long and pale, with dark hair plastered down on the forehead, soaking wet. She couldn't make out the features on the face that well; he might be young or old or somewhere in between.

He was dripping, it looked like. Or maybe that was just the distortion of the glass.

The worst thing was that his lips were moving. She couldn't hear what he was saying, but his lips were moving. And as they moved she felt a kind of coldness come over her, moving up from the soles of her feet like it was radiating from the floor.... It was a sick cold, the cold of lonely graves, the cold of a hospital bed that you knew, in the pit of your stomach, you would never leave....

"You have to open it," whispered Jax. "He won't leave otherwise."

"No way, Jax," she whispered back. "No way, no way, no way."

"You have to," he said.

"Jax, honestly," she said. Her teeth were chattering, her feet were freezing, and she hugged herself. "I always believe you. But this is some guy on our steps in the night. He could be a murderer."

"He could," said Jax. "But he's not here for that."

"Well, that's a comfort," she said.

"He's like all the dark things," said Jax. "He can't come in unless you invite him."

"You promise?"

"Well…I think so. OK, so I'm not a hundred percent sure."

She hesitated, conflicted. Then she looked down at his worried face and thought of him by himself in his bed, hugging his knees to his spindly chest and waiting for their mother.

This was about showing Jax she trusted him. And that he hadn't been abandoned.

Reluctantly, squeezing her eyes shut, she turned the lock and pulled open the door.

And when she opened her eyes again, she had to clap a hand to her mouth to stifle a shriek.

The screen was still closed, but there was only the thin mesh between them and him. And now she saw what she hadn't been able to see from the other side of the glass: he wasn't just wet. He was pouring.

Water was running from his hair down his dark coat, dripping from his nose and ears and chin. Water pooled at his feet. It dripped off the ends of his sleeves, down his front, down his legs. It coursed over his face steadily.

And it wasn't the rain. A light drizzle was falling behind him, beyond the porch. But under the porch, the visitor had a roof over his head.

And yet the water kept sliding down his face.

The man's mouth was still moving, but there was no sound. It moved the same way again and again, like he was repeating himself.

The water poured off him and his lips moved, on and on. And the cold sickness suffused her, rose in a wave through her body until it felt deafening....

"Jax," she whispered, struggling against it. "Do you know what he's saying?"

There was no answer from Jax till she turned to look at him. He was staring at the man, the man he said wasn't a person at all.

The Pouring Man.

"*Where is she,*" said Jax tonelessly. "*Where is she.*"

Cara couldn't help herself. She grabbed the door and slammed it.

The bang reverberated through the sleeping house.

She stood there shivering uncontrollably.

Behind them someone spoke.

"What's going on?"

Both of them jumped, squealing.

But it was only Max, standing at the top of the stairs in his boxers, hair all tousled and sticking up. He looked like a cranky, messy version of James Franco.

"You woke me up! It's the middle of the night! What is it, man?"

They looked at each other. They were still breathing hard, still trembling.

"Uh, sorry, Max," said Cara.

"I couldn't sleep," mumbled Jax.

"Just keep it down, would you?" said Max grumpily, and shambled back toward his bedroom.

They waited a minute, until they heard his room door close.

"Is he gone?" asked Cara, in a low voice.

Jax knew who she meant.

"Not yet," he said.

Slowly, with butterflies in her stomach, she turned back to the diamond pane in the door. It was just inches from her face. She leaned forward bit by bit and looked out.

There he was.

Close.

Closer.

Right there.

His white face with dark hollows of eyes.

The lips still working, working.

Where is she.

"Go away," said Cara. It was almost a whimper.

And then, just like that, his face vanished.

"*Now* he's gone," said Jax calmly.

They decided to share her room. Jax pulled his sleeping bag right up onto her bed, on top of the covers, and she felt the weight of his small body. She turned to face in the same direction and draped her arm over his side.

Outside, the Pouring Man wanted their mother.

He was *looking* for their mother.

That was what he had meant by *Where is she*. Cara was sure. On that point, she didn't have to ask Jax.

She thought she'd never go to sleep, she was so confused. She felt kind of dazzled, in fact, as though something she couldn't understand had been flashed in her face. A side of the world she'd never seen.

A shadow world beneath this one.

Where is she. The water pouring off of him.

It was a black whirlwind. But at the same time, deep inside it, there was a kernel of new hope…because maybe this was a sign that her mother really hadn't just left their dad, or left *them*. That there was something else at work.

Something hidden.

Three

The smell of pancakes and melting butter wafted up to her room in the morning and brought her out of a half-suffocating dream of ice and a big white face. She jiggled the mattress as she got out of bed, waking up Jax. Pancakes were one of their dad's few edible recipes; this time of year he put in fresh blueberries, which he bought at a roadside stand in front of a cranberry bog on 6.

"Wait," said Jax, sitting up and rubbing his eyes with his fists. "I gotta come down with you."

She went to the bathroom sink to brush her teeth and splash cold water on her face.

"You're not shtill...*shensing* him, are you?"

She had a mouthful of toothpaste.

"I just have to check on something," he said, and climbed out of the bed.

In his dinosaur pajamas (none too clean, with threadbare patches between the legs) and dangling his old stuffed animal (a mangy-looking giraffe), it was hard to match the words and attitude that came out of him with his little-kid face and body.

She loved him a lot, but Jax was definitely a puzzle.

"Check what?" she asked curiously.

"It's just a hunch." And he went out her bedroom door, depositing his giraffe unceremoniously on the floor.

"Wait up!" she called after him, and leaned over the sink to spit out the toothpaste froth.

When she got to the bottom of the stairs he had the front door of the house open. and the screen door, too. She heard satellite radio playing behind her in the kitchen, a droning voice with a British accent; her dad liked to listen to the BBC World News as he flipped pancakes. She saw Jax bending down to stare at the porch's old slats, whose white paint was scuffed and faded.

She went outside to join him. On the top step there was a puddle of water.

That was all. A puddle.

"Don't touch it," said Jax.

"Are you kidding? What is it, poisoned or something?"

"Something," said Jax grimly. "Don't let Dad or Max come out here. And get me a cloth to soak it up with, OK? A thick one."

"Yes, sir," said Cara, and ducked into the ground-floor bathroom, stealing a glance into the kitchen as she passed the door. Max was on a stool at the island, scarfing pancakes—he had a big appetite these days—and her dad wasn't looking in their direction. She grabbed a bath towel from the rack.

On the steps, Jax dropped it carefully so that half stayed dry while the other half soaked up the puddle.

"See, we don't want it tracked into the house," he said. "We want it to evaporate before anyone steps on it. I was hoping it would already be gone, but humidity's pretty high today. Here." And he picked up the towel gingerly and handed it to Cara, who took hold of it by the dry corners. "Hang it in the sun somewhere. Somewhere the others won't touch it."

She walked around to the back of the house, facing the bay, and carefully hung the towel up on a line between two trees where her mother sometimes dried the sheets. She felt slightly foolish doing it, as though she was humoring Jax in a bizarre delusion.

Then she had a strong picture of the Pouring Man's face, how it had come closer—closer—closer into the frame of the front-door window. It hadn't happened gradually, like a person walking toward you, but more in sudden jumps.

Far.

Nearer.

VERY NEAR.

If Jax was seeing things, so was she.

"So," he was saying to their dad and Max when she came in the back door, standing at the kitchen island holding his glass of orange juice, "no one went out onto the porch this morning?"

"Nah," said Max, "why?"

"Oh, I—I think I dropped my stylus out there."

"It's probably right where you left it," said their dad soothingly. "Two pancakes or three?"

"Three," said Jax and Cara together.

53

"Three more for me too," said Max.

"I've raised a herd of feral hogs," said their dad.

❊

After they loaded the dishes into the dishwasher Cara and Jax held a council in his room, which was good for privacy since both her dad and Max were reluctant to set foot inside due to snail, frog, and crab hazards.

"So why did you think—how did you know there was something wrong with the water?"

"I don't know for sure, but we have to be careful is all," said Jax. "That puddle could easily have been tainted. He can control water, Car. You know how both times we've seen him it's been in the rain? Or with water just—like streaming down off him?"

"Uh-huh," said Cara.

She got it. He was the Pouring Man.

"It's his element. As in, ancient Greek element? Air, earth, water, or fire? Not as in the Periodic Table."

She wasn't certain what he meant but nodded anyway. If you stopped Jax every time you weren't quite sure what he was talking about, you'd never finish a conversation.

"Water is his element and night's his best time, probably because it tends to be more humid then. Who knows what he can do with water? A lot, I suspect. And we don't want any part of him in our house, that's for sure. Water is his power *and* his constraint."

54

"Talk normally."

"His limit. He can only move freely where there's a certain amount of water present, and it's easier for him at night. It's how he is."

"But if there's no signal to read, how do you know all this?"

"That's actually a good question," said Jax in a know-it-all way, as though he were her teacher.

As he talked, he was lifting a frog out of his terrarium, one finger on each of its sides, its thin back legs dangling.

"He sends me messages, right? Last night, he *wanted* us to see him. He wanted us to hear the question. The question *Where is she.* And if we'd known the answer, trust me, he'd know it now, too. So it's just as well that we didn't."

"Wait. You mean he can know what we're thinking? Like—he can ping us?"

Jax opened his window and set the frog out on the roof, where it hopped away toward a tree branch.

"Is that a *tree* frog?" asked Cara. "Because—"

"He can read me, at least," said Jax, turning back to her. "I'm not sure if he can read you or not."

"How about—the stuff about the water? He told you that too?"

"No. That stuff—I just knew it. The way you know what up or down means, but it's hard to describe them without using the words *up* or *down*. See what I'm saying?"

"Kind of," said Cara uncertainly.

She half wished Max or Hayley were here, to make Jax explain things in a more basic way. Or just so she didn't feel like she was the only one whose head was spinning.

"It doesn't seem empirically verifiable," said Jax. "Any of it. I realize that."

"Uh, yeah," said Cara.

"But Car, I promise you. It's real."

He said this softly. He'd sat back down on his bed, opposite her, and his scrawny legs were crossed in front of him. Jax always managed to have scabs on his knees and bruises on his shins.

"I guess, if I'm gonna go with this," she said slowly, "I have to stop second-guessing you. It's kind of like I have to either believe it all or believe none of it. Otherwise I'll just keep feeling like my head is going to explode."

"Like the posters from that old TV show," said Jax, and nodded solemnly. "Remember? *I Want to Believe.*"

"Mmm," murmured Cara. Actually it was more like she had to suspend disbelief—a term from English class. "But what does he have to do with her? I mean, how could Mom be connected to a scary—whatever he is? And why is he looking for her?"

"I don't have those answers yet," said Jax, and shook his head. "But I did remember something. The leatherback? In the writing on your driftwood?"

"Yeah? What about it?"

"They have one at Woods Hole—at the Aquarium. They got it recently. It hasn't been there for long. Mom was telling me about it though, how she wanted me to come see it. But then she…."

He trailed off. *Then she vanished.*

After a second Cara spoke.

"You think that could be the one in the message?"

"I don't have any other ideas," said Jax. "I mean, how many leatherbacks can there be on the Cape? Unless we want to head for the open ocean, that is."

"Then we need to come up with an excuse to get Dad to drive us there," she said.

⚏

It was Jax who invented the pretext: a flash drive he claimed must have been left in their mother's desk, with some of his data. Their dad wasn't happy about it, but Jax played on his heartstrings. Cara suggested they could combine it with a trip to the Aquarium, which was in the building next door.

At the last minute, as they were getting into the car, Max appeared on his skateboard, flipping it up into his hand right before he hit the sandy stretch of their street. He jumped into the backseat next to Jax, his board tucked under his arm.

It was a new one, Cara noticed—flames and a grinning skull. Really cute.

"Slide over," he ordered him. "I got long legs."

"You're coming?" asked Cara.

"You kidding? Miss the dogfish swimming around in the dirty water? And the quahogs that look so yummy? Forget it."

Cara didn't like to eat quahogs, or anything slimy that came from the sea. When she had to watch people slurping oysters in restaurants, she felt like throwing up.

Maybe she shouldn't plan on bussing tables after all.

"Didn't expect you back so soon," said their dad to Max as they pulled away from the house.

"This scuffle broke out at the park," said Max mildly.

He meant the skatepark, near the pier.

"You were *fighting*?" asked their dad.

"Not me," said Max. "I had to break it up, sorta."

Max was hardly ever on one side or the other. He was the kind of guy who got along with all the groups at school but wasn't really a part of any of them: the jocks, the geeks, the stoner types. He was kind of a free agent, which was hard to carry off if you also wanted to be popular. But somehow Max did it.

"What happened?" asked their dad, flicking on his right-turn signal as they reached Route 6.

"Oh, you know," said Max, shrugging. "What always happens. Nothing much. Two guys with supersized egos. Name-calling, whatever. It wasn't too bad, maybe a sprained wrist was all that happened. Anyway, I just wasn't in the mood after, so I figured I'd cut out. No biggie."

Cara glanced back at Jax, who was looking at Max admiringly. Max was a hero of Jax's but had no idea his little

brother worshiped him. In fact, Max thought *Jax* thought
he was stupid. Which made him come down hard on Jax
sometimes. Especially lately.

"That's cool," said Jax, trying to sound cool himself.

Max shrugged again, settled back in his seat and stuck
in his buds.

When they finally got to Woods Hole, Cara was
relieved: her dad had taken advantage of the long car ride
to deliver a lecture on the Protestant Reformation—mostly
to her, since Jax was typing on his smartphoneand Max was
listening to *London Calling* (with the volume cranked up
so high that she was practically listening to *London Calling*
too). Her dad tried to spice up the lesson with details about
how Martin Luther got married to a nun he smuggled out
of her nunnery in a stinky fish barrel, but that part sounded
made up and the rest was a bit on the snoozy side.

They drove through hilly, tree-lined neighborhoods and
out into the town, which was arranged around a harbor-
front, with restaurants and bars built right onto the pilings
and a big salt pond set back from the shore in the middle of
the ocean institute's buildings.

"Let's do the Aquarium thing first," said Max when
they'd all climbed out of the car and stretched.

Jax and Cara exchanged looks.

"There's no rush on the thumb drive, I guess," said Jax.

"How about I'll go check the office for you, Jax," said
Cara. "I'm better at finding things. You guys can hang with
the seals or whatever."

Jax nodded. "OK with me."

"I'll let you in, Cara," said their dad from the driver's seat. "I've got her keys somewhere in here." And he fiddled with the door to the glove compartment.

"See you in a few," said Max, and he and Jax split off toward the Aquarium entrance.

Cara hadn't thought it would affect her the way it did, being inside her mother's office. But as soon as her dad unlocked the door and opened it for her ("Take your time, honey, I'm going to step down the hall and talk to Roger") she felt overwhelmed. The feeling washed over her that her mother had been with them a long, long time ago.

And that long-ago time might never be coming back.

Her knees went weak and she had to sit down in her mother's desk chair.

As she sat there, a strange feeling of mixed dread and anticipation trilling though her, she looked around slowly. The office wasn't much different from how she remembered it; the only sign of anything out of the ordinary was a dried-out plant that had dropped some dead leaves. No one had bothered to water it.

"You got your kids with you?" Roger was asking her dad in the hall, friendly. "The boy genius?"

"Jax is over at the Aquarium," answered her dad.

There were the framed pictures of all of them on the desk, which seemed pretty neat and well-organized considering how many stacks of reports there were. Her mother wasn't in any of the pictures, Cara realized, because she had always been the one taking them.

She was just killing time; Jax had given her a thumb drive to show their dad, pretending she'd found it when she was ready to go. Through the open office door she could hear him saying hello to Roger. Roger was one of her mother's colleagues—an older biologist type who was more or less the boss, as far as Cara could tell.

She opened and closed drawers, then took a tour of the keepsakes on the edges of the bookshelves. Miniature seals and sea lions, dolphins and walruses carved out of bone... Out in the hall, her dad and Roger were getting closer and harder and harder to ignore.

"This kind of occurrence is unprecedented here," Roger was saying, sounding worried. "To actually have data stolen—I mean her drive was wiped clean."

"And this was the, what—this was the work on ocean acidification? Effects on shellfish, trophic ramifications?" asked her dad.

"She was slated to testify before Congress," said Roger. "Of course, that was before...but this break-in only happened two days ago. I was going to call you. Only reason it was discovered was one of her grad students was working late, saw her door open, went in, and found the hard drive busy erasing itself. Someone had programmed it to do so, obviously. Every printout that was back from peer review was gone too, but copies of the article are still floating around. It's the original dataset that's missing. And without it..."

"But why would anyone *do that*?" asked her dad.

The two of them were at the door now, her dad shaking his head.

"The research is important," said Roger. "It has major political impact, potentially. This was the first data to show conclusively that the ocean food chain is beginning to collapse from higher acidity and will crash completely if CO_2 emissions aren't curbed. First the calcium-carbonate forming organisms will die off, plankton, pteropods, shellfish of all kinds, every species of coral. Her sample showed actual evidence of that beginning to happen. Then the species that depend on *those* organisms for food will start to crash, and of course that's where her interest originated: marine mammals."

"Yes I know, we talked about it," said Cara's dad. "She was deeply concerned."

"Fish stocks will collapse. Macroalgae could force out what's left of the coral reefs, already bleaching and stressed. Cyanobacteria and dinoflagellates could rise. The oceans as we know them could virtually die off...."

The men were silent for a long moment. Then Roger cleared his throat.

"My point is, if she hadn't—disappeared, for lack of a better term—she was going to Washington, DC to testify on this."

"So you're saying, with this break-in—you think maybe someone actually might have—*taken* her?"

His tone made Cara's pulse quicken, so she moved away from the door, picking up a small box from the desk, mostly to occupy her shaking hands. It was decorated with spiral designs and made of a white, pearly material. Idly, trying not to hear the conversation, she slid the top open.

"...can't believe anyone would go to those lengths," came Roger's voice. "It's not like she's the only one studying this. New data are being gathered constantly."

"Then what happened, Roger?" asked Cara's dad in an urgent tone. "Where *is* she?"

Inside the box, Cara saw, was a small piece of rolled-up paper. She uncurled it.

What had he meant, "taken"?

There was some kind of poem on the paper, though she couldn't focus on it at the moment.

The night of fires beneath the sea...

"Cara? You ready, honey?" came her dad's voice.

"Sure," she said hastily, and stuffed paper and box into her shoulder bag. "Coming."

"Find what you were looking for?" he asked.

They were walking together to the elevator over the slick linoleum.

But he was distracted and not really listening.

"Dad," she said slowly. "I heard what you guys were saying. Someone hacked into Mom's computer, right? When you said maybe she was 'taken,' did you mean kidnapped?"

"Oh, sweetheart," said her dad. "No, no. Look. I was just throwing out ideas. The truth is, that's preposterous.

We don't live inside a great conspiracy theory, after all. I'm just—just trying to figure out our situation. And you're helping me. Right?"

He clapped her reassuringly on the shoulder, but he seemed to be somewhere else entirely.

⋇⋇⋇

Her dad took a walk around the village harbor while she went to find Max and Jax. She went by the Aquarium's outdoor tank with the seals and through the front doors, stopping only to sign in. She passed the row of tanks holding blue lobsters, the ugly, snaggle-toothed wolffish and the conger eels; the place was practically empty today.

Her brothers were probably upstairs, she thought, where the holding tanks were—the part of the Aquarium the management called "behind the scenes," though it was open to the public like the rest and really just rougher and messier looking, with more cement and metal and exposed pipes and stuff. She took the stairs up and then stopped.

A few feet away, near the long, shallow tray table that held the animals kids were allowed to touch, stood Jax, gazing into a tank that held a massive turtle.

The leatherback, she guessed.

Opposite him the turtle floated in the tank's brackish-looking water with its beak almost up to the glass and its large flippers moving slowly. It was huge—almost as big as a person. Cara couldn't see its eyes; they seemed to blend into its black-and-white-spotted body. It was a strange-looking sea turtle, not like others she'd seen—streamlined and more graceful. It didn't seem to have a real shell on its back at all, only the dark hide with ridges in it.

It was quiet in the room. All she could hear was the buzzing and bubbling of the tanks' filters and the constant soft trickling of their water.

A sign on the tank said LEATHERBACK SEA TURTLE. RESCUE ANIMAL BEING REHABILITATED FOR RE-RELEASE. THIS SPECIES IS ROUGHLY 110 MILLION YEARS OLD.

Jax and the sea turtle were face-to-face.

That in itself wasn't so unbelievable. What was harder to fathom—and Cara was used to mysterious events occurring when Jax was around—was the stream that seemed to flow between them, like a turbulence in the air. If you weren't watching closely you might not see it, or if you did see it you might just assume it was an optical illusion or some kind of minor air disturbance, an interruption in the atmosphere. It reminded her of heat waves hovering over a long road in the desert—the rippling transparency some people called a mirage.

Cara had caught sight of it once or twice before, when Jax was reading someone and there was an especially strong connection. At first she'd thought it was some kind of mirage herself, until Jax explained it had to do with the signal and was a "thermal perturbation."

But she'd never seen it between Jax and an animal.

And never this visible or this clear.

As far as she knew, Jax had only ever been able to read people. He didn't, for instance, have a clue what Rufus was thinking—ever. Or identify too strongly with the frogs and crabs he brought into his room. That was obvious.

It was something about the human cerebral cortex, he had suggested once to her, maybe its size or thickness— about the structure of the brain or language, she thought she remembered him saying.

But here he was, talking to a turtle.

Good thing the Aquarium was so empty, she thought, looking around at the room's leaking, rusty pipes and concrete walkways with the rubber mats on them. She wondered what the general public would think of the scene: a blond boy with dirty fingernails, his phone clutched in one hand, leaning his small face toward the beaked, hooded face of a turtle that hovered a couple of feet away from him and was contained behind glass.

Around the turtle, in its watery enclosure, dark reddish seaweed waved.

And a few feet behind Jax—one of his hands dragging unnoticed in the touching tank near a baby octopus, where he seemed to have forgotten it—was Max.

Looking thunderstruck. Staring.

Max had always dismissed the idea that Jax could read people. "No offense," he liked to say, "but I'm a skeptic."

"What the hell," he said now to Cara, his voice lowered. He snatched his hand out of the tank. "Is he—like, OK?"

"Jax?" said Cara. "*What is it?*"

"I don't know," said Jax uncertainly. "It's—the turtle's talking to me."

"Yeah, right," said Max sarcastically in the background.

"He's—it's not like the Pouring Man, is he?" asked Cara. "Where he's all blank? But he can get into your head?"

Jax shook his head.

"No, not at all," he whispered. "Not at all. There's a signal, like with a person. And it's not a he, it's a she."

"What did you say? The *foreign man*?" asked Max.

"Kids!" called their dad, coming up the stairs behind Cara. "Time to get going."

〰

Max insisted that Cara share the backseat with him on the way home. She hadn't had a chance yet to ask Jax what had happened—for instance, why on earth a turtle whose ancestors had been around for about 110 million years would want to shoot the breeze with a ten-year-old kid whose worn-out stegosaurus pajamas had gaping crotch holes.

Or whether the turtle had anything to say about their mother.

But Max was getting his chance to grill *her*.

"First off," said Max into her ear, so her dad couldn't hear him, "what was that—what was that, like, *stream* moving through the air? You know what I'm talking about."

"I thought you were a skeptic," she muttered.

"I'm totally a skeptic," he hissed. "But I have eyes. I saw something. So what the hell was it?"

"Jax once said it was a thermal perturbation," she said. "Don't ask me what that means. But it's what happens when he reads a signal. With people. And he can tell, more or less, what they're…"

"…thinking," finished Max.

"Basically."

"OK, so let's just say I believe Jax can—well, that Jax has some way of knowing what people are thinking, sometimes. Let's just say, hypothetically, I may have suspected something like that once or twice. Still: this was a *turtle*. And a big mofo, too."

"I noticed."

"So, you're trying to tell me he was reading the turtle's mind? My little brother was hanging out doing some kind of ESP action on a reptile. That's what you want me to believe."

"I don't want you to believe *any*thing," whispered Cara fiercely. "But it'd be nice if you could be more open-minded, I guess."

"One man's open-minded is another man's crazy as a bedbug," said Max.

Cara shook her head and held up her phone, erasing old texts for something to do. It was no use talking to people who didn't want to hear.

After a few minutes Max relented.

"Hey, I know something was really going on back there," he said awkwardly. "It's just hard to…"

"Suspend disbelief," said Cara.

He nodded.

"And what about this—what did you call him? Foreign man?—"

"Pouring man," said Cara.

"—who you said could get into Jax's head? What was that all about?"

She hesitated, wondering how much to tell him. In the front seat, Jax and her dad were talking about "carbon storage" and "echinoderms"—nothing she really understood. She loved Jax and she loved her dad, but sometimes she felt like their smart-club only had room for two members. In a way she had more in common with Max, who was at least down to earth. Unlike Jax or her dad, both she and Max would rather go for a walk on the beach or to a party than, say, find a nice empty room and get cozy with a copy of *The Rise and Fall of the Roman Empire* or *Relativity: The Special and the General Theory.*

She might as well give it a shot. Even if he didn't believe her about the Pouring Man, what did she have to lose? This whole summer, when she needed him most, he'd barely been able to spare her the time of day.

So it couldn't get much worse than it already was.

"You're not going to believe me if I tell you," she said.

"Yeah," allowed Max, "you're probably right. But tell me anyway."

So she did.

She and Jax didn't have any time alone during the afternoon, since her dad was taking the day to spend "quality time" with his younger son; then, right after dinner, Hayley showed up with a cake her mother had baked for them. Hayley's mother was divorced and clearly believed that that was what was happening in Cara's family, too.

It was annoying to Cara that Hayley's mom thought she knew more about Cara's own family than they did. But at least there was an upside: homemade desserts, once every week since June.

So they all hung out on the porch, Cara sitting with Hayley on the swing, the others in lawn chairs and on the front steps, eating their pieces of cake as dark descended. They talked about normal stuff—the guys fighting at the skatepark, school starting up again.

The guys went inside one by one as they finished their cake, first her dad, then Max, and finally Jax, till she and Hayley were just going back and forth slowly, listening to the swing creak. Cara figured she was stuck there, for a few minutes at least—she needed to debrief Jax, but she couldn't just dump Hayley. She thought about telling her friend about the Pouring Man, the turtle, all of it, but she couldn't decide.

She wanted to confide in her; on the other hand, she didn't want to scare her. Ever since her mom and dad got divorced and her dad moved to Idaho or somewhere, Hayley got scared by strange men. So did her mom, come to think of it. Cara wasn't sure exactly why—maybe something about the divorce itself, which had been pretty mean—but it probably wasn't the time to delve into the subject.

And she hadn't believed Cara about the driftwood, anyway.

After Hayley left, she climbed the stairs quickly, impatient to ask Jax what was up with the turtle. But when she knocked on his door there was no answer. She pushed open the door and saw he was fast asleep: his moon light shone down from the wall, and the stuffed giraffe lay in the crook of one arm. He was so exhausted he hadn't even managed to change into the dreaded pajamas.

She thought about waking him up, but he looked so wiped out she couldn't bring herself to.

Alone in her own bedroom, she took the small white box from her bag, the box she'd found in her mother's office, and unrolled the yellowing scroll.

The night of fires beneath the sea
Among the bones of the Whydahlee
Three must visit the old selkie:
Interpreter, arbiter, and visionary.

Only then may the bonds come undone,
The fourth secure'd of fear's venom;
The man who walks in water gone,
A path laid out for the absent one.

It sounded like some kind of prophesy, she thought. Did it have something to do with the turtle, with the driftwood message?

Was it their mother talking to them?

It wasn't her mother's handwriting, though, and she didn't think her mother wrote poems; her mother was a scientist. Plus the paper looked old.

Then again, obviously, it had been in her mother's office....

The man who walks in water. The Pouring Man. It had to be!

And this had to be meant for them.

She would show it to Jax first thing in the morning.

And Max. What about him? She wasn't sure what he was thinking. She had told him everything; he had listened, but, though he hadn't made fun of her openly, he made no sign of buying into what she was saying, either. When she was done he had nodded without commenting, turned away from her, and looked out at the other cars passing them.

"'Three must visit the old selkie, interpreter, arbiter and visionary,'" she read aloud, softly.

Just then something hit the glass of her window, which was half-open. She almost jumped out of her skin. Slowly, and wishing she wasn't alone, she got up. She walked over to where the curtains were billowing inward and then, after a long moment of held breath, jerked them apart.

She couldn't see anything, not even the trees outside, because her eyes were adjusted to the bright, artificial lighting of her room. There was no noise from anywhere, though, and she was still curious, so she decided to dig her pen-sized flashlight out of her desk.

There were a few beads of moisture on the glass where the object had hit, and through the mesh of the screen below she could see a small dark pile of something, lying on the porch roof just beneath her windowsill. Dead leaves, she thought, maybe—but why had they hit the window? There was no wind.

She raised the screen to see them better—she was nervous but felt like she needed to know. She leaned over with the penlight's beam sharply focused.

It was a cluster of dark-brown packets that looked like seaweed: shiny, black rectangles with thorny-looking ends. She had found pouches like these on the beach many times and knew what they were: skate egg cases that people sometimes called "mermaid's purses." Skates were like rays, her mother had taught her—carnivorous rays that slithered over the ocean floor.

So these were just skate eggs, right? A frequent find for beachcombers?

Though you didn't usually encounter them on the roof. At night. Outside your bedroom window.

Skates didn't fly, after all.

She reached out to push them away, then jerked her hand back. She remembered what Jax had said: the Pouring Man controlled water, and you had to make sure you didn't invite him in.

She stuck her head and shoulders out over the window ledge, her elbows on the shingles of the porch roof, and held the penlight over the mass of eggs. Steadily, steadily. Before she even touched them to push them away she should make sure they were what they seemed to be.

For a long moment she held the spot of the penlight in one place, shining into the brown translucence of an egg pouch, and noticed nothing unusual.

Then she saw the squirming.

Inside the pouch, small things squirmed and pulsed. Their movement was rapid…as if they were about to burst out.

And whatever was inside them, she didn't think it wasn't baby skates. Unless skates had claws.

In a shudder of revulsion she stretched out her penlight and pushed the egg pouches with it, once, then again. She couldn't touch it with her own fingers, but she knew she had to get it away. Get rid of it.

She stretched farther and farther onto the roof. The egg pouches didn't roll down by themselves—the grade of the roof wasn't steep enough—so she had to keep pushing and prodding them toward the edge. Finally her whole body was outside her bedroom window, with her feet hooked around the inside ledge of the sill, and she was quickly prodding the cluster farther and farther toward the edge. It seemed to be moving more frantically now, like the eggs would hatch any second. She shivered in disgust as she flicked it away from her.

One last push—stretching, stretching, almost letting go with her feet—and the brown mass protruded over the gutter, caught a bit on the gutter's outer lip, and finally tumbled off the edge.

She stayed there for a minute, slowing her breathing. Then she let the penlight roll out of her grasp. She didn't want it in her room either, not after it had touched *that*.

She heard a clink as it rolled off the shingles and into the gutter.

Once she was back inside she closed her window and pulled the curtains closed again. Climbed into her bed and pulled the coverlet all the way up to her chin.

Her room door was open, and it creaked as it opened wider. She gasped and sat bolt upright in her bed.

But it was only Rufus.

"I'm so glad you're here," she told him.

Four

She and Max came out of their rooms into the upstairs hall at exactly the same time in the morning. It was early; she was surprised to see him. Usually he liked to hole up in his room till 11 on weekend mornings, headphones securely engaged.

"What can I say," said Max, and grinned. "Curiosity and felines."

They stood at Jax's door and Cara knocked. When Jax didn't open it they went in. A window was open, as usual, curtains fluttering in the breeze, but Jax was nowhere to be seen.

"Wait," said Max. "There's something else missing."

Jax's terrarium was gone, and so were his two saltwater tanks. In fact, his whole room appeared to be wildlife-free.

"No way," said Cara.

They went down the stairs together; Max peeled off for the front yard while she went through the kitchen to the back. Past the clothesline, where the towel from the Pouring Man's puddle still hung, through the pitch pines and bear oak, down onto the marshy shoreline. Past the patch of grass beneath her room where the skate eggs must have fallen— the eggs that were not skates but something else instead.

But there was nothing there.

The tide was low.

And there was Jax, looking absurd in nothing but big rubber boots and baggy blue swim trunks, his bare stomach and ribs smeared with dirt. He stood at the water's edge, and a few feet behind him in the reedy mud were his tanks, tipped over and empty.

She wondered if it was dangerous, so near the water. But then, Jax had said the Pouring Man moved best at night, and it was daytime now.

"What's going on?" asked Cara.

"Just releasing them," he said. "They're animals, you know. Wild animals don't enjoy captivity."

"Uh-huh," said Max, coming up behind Cara. "So that's what the turtle did? Sang you the theme song from *Born Free*?"

That was a famous but boring old movie their mother made them watch, about training a tame lion to go back in the wild again. Totally seventies, but Jax loved it.

"No, the turtle, as you call her," said Jax with some dignity, "was far less juvenile than you are."

"Whoa-ho," said Max. "Testy."

"Really, Jax," said Cara. "We're dying to know, here. Did she—communicate something?"

Jax looked at Max, and then back at her.

"I told him," she said.

"She said we have to go underwater," said Jax after a few seconds, and sloshed through the shallows to pick up a plastic cup. He poured it out gently, and Cara thought she saw minnows glitter in the falling stream. "She said we have to watch the sea, and when the sea—lights up at night, I guess it was?—we have to go in. And if everything goes right, a friend of hers will help us."

"Help us what," said Max flatly.

"Help us to get Mom back."

Cara was still a moment, her flip-slops sinking into the mud. Then she pulled up her feet with a sucking sound.

"*The night of fires beneath the sea*," she murmured.

"Yes," said Jax, looking at her sharply. "That's what she said! How did you know?"

"I found a message in Mom's office. It reads like a clue. Either that or a prediction or something."

"And how are we supposed to go, uh, underwater? Last I checked, you and Cara didn't know scuba," said Max, who did.

"So maybe you need to teach us."

"Get out," said Max. "Seriously, get out. You're too young, and I'm not even fully certified myself. Remember?"

For a second the three of them stood there, in the mud and the water, an awkward triangle.

"Let's cross that bridge later," said Cara. "OK?"

"Look," said Max. "I'll keep my doubts to myself on most of this, but as far as going scuba diving with maybe a few days' prep from someone who's not even certified, it would be irresponsible. I can't stand by and watch my baby brother get an embolism because of a bad tip a, like, *zoo animal* gave him through mental telepathy."

"She's not a zoo animal," retorted Jax. "She's a wild leatherback, *Dermochelys coriacea*, the largest of all turtles and the only living species in her genus. They're critically endangered, which means one of her is worth roughly 300,000 of you."

"Hey, thanks a lot for the show of support," said Max.

"Plus, she was caught in a fishing net and almost died and they nursed her back to health," said Jax, stiff.

"But Jax," said Cara, "you've never been able to read *animals*. You don't go around talking to pets or anything. So how did you do it?"

"I don't know, but there was something different about her," said Jax, softening slightly. "*Dermochelys* is one aspect of her, but not all aspects. That's all I get right now."

"So you're not gonna be having deep talks with Rufus, then," said Max.

"This was an individual with a special capacity," said Jax.

"Phew, that's a relief," said Max.

"But there *are* more of them."

"More talking turtles?" asked Max.

"More like her, whatever she is. I'll know them when I see them."

I'll know them when I see them, thought Cara. *See. See. Vision. Visionary.* Interpreter, arbiter and *visionary*. She'd have to look up the other words from the message; "interpreter" was easy, but "arbiter" she didn't know. Or "selkie."

80

Faintly they heard the telltale *bang* of the screen door. Probably their dad stepping out onto the porch, stretching and bending down for the Sunday paper.

"Here, little dude," said Max. "Let me help you with these," and he picked up Jax's terrarium to carry it back into the house.

❄❅

They met in Max's bedroom next, and he turned on his usual loud music—this time to disguise the conversation. It was the Ramones, something violent about beating up rats with a baseball bat.

Cara told them both about the skate eggs, which made Max shrug and Jax look perplexed, though definitely not as alarmed as she had been.

"I guess you had to be there," she ended up saying, when neither of them had much of a response. "So here's the message." And she unfurled the small scroll and read it out loud.

They were silent for a while after she stopped.

"Well, that's clear as mud," said Max.

Jax cocked his head.

"So first off," said Max, "it sounds like we have to find out *when* the seas are going to light up. Which—I mean, who the hell knows how we do that?"

"We have to wait and see," said Jax. "Watch and wait. Wait and see."

"Second, where is this meeting actually supposed to be? The poem, or whatever it is, said 'sea.' Which covers, oh, about two-thirds of the Earth's surface last time I counted. So that doesn't really, uh, *pinpoint* a location," said Max.

"She told me where to look," said Jax.

"She?" asked Cara.

"The turtle. She said there's a finger that points to it."

"A finger that points to it," repeated Max. "Uh-huh."

"That's what she said. We have to find the finger and look where it's pointing," said Jax. "And that's where we watch for the fires."

"Man, hope it's not the middle one," said Max.

"How droll," said Jax. "Quite humorous."

"Whatever, you two go ahead. Find the *finger*," said Max. "But then there's still a problem. I mean, even if we figure out those two deals, there's still the question of what we're supposed to do. Once we get underwater. I mean I have no clue what any of that gibberish is supposed to mean."

"*Three must visit the old selkie…*," mused Cara. "I think the three clearly means us. And I just looked up 'selkie' in dad's big dictionary, and it's supposed to be some kind of mythic creature that turns from a seal into a woman or something. So maybe the turtle's friend is a seal?"

"And who are the Whydahlee?" asked Jax. "And their bones…is it like an Indian burial ground?"

"Who knows?" said Max, making a face. "Not exactly ol' Bill Shakespeare, is it."

"Why don't you take that one," said Cara. "For now, Jax and I will try to find out where in the sea we're looking. And you try to find out who Whydah Lee is, where she's buried or whatever. OK?"

"And how should I do that? Ask around?"

"Like, you could start by just googling Whydah Lee or something."

"True," said Max. "When in doubt, google."

"We'll leave the underwater fires till later," said Cara. "That one does seem kind of vague."

She and Jax set off on their bikes by mid-morning, knapsacks on their back holding bottles filled with melting ice cubes and a couple of chocolate bars they'd picked up at a gas station convenience store. They headed for a spot in the next village along, called Eastham, inside the national seashore. Jax said he thought they would find the finger there.

They coasted along the curving, tree-shaded streets of Eastham after they crossed Route 6, calling back and forth.

"So—I don't get it," said Cara. "If she could tell you where to find the finger, why couldn't she just tell you where in the ocean we're supposed to look? Isn't it, like, adding an extra step? I hate when they do that in stories."

"She just didn't trust me to know what she was talking about," said Jax. "It was easier for her to tell me where the finger was because it's on land. Because I know this place.

But I don't know the ocean and it's so huge and she couldn't give me a picture of the location because it's just under waves that all look the same. A needle-in-a-haystack-type thing."

They rode up a street that climbed a hill past an old fort and locked their bikes on to a rack in a small parking lot. From up here, on top of the aptly named Fort Hill, they could see a sweeping vista below—the grassy marsh with its blue channels cutting through it, the lagoon, and a long, thin barrier island that protected the beach. The ocean looked very blue beneath the green fields of the headland.

Near where they left their bikes, a trail led along the shoreline, past meadows of wildflowers (and poison ivy; you always had to watch out for that). It wended its way through a swamp full of red maples, where sometimes Cara had seen tiny voles and shrews peeking out of holes in the ground.

Jax led her along the swamp trail, through the trees, and then over some raised wooden walkways where the mud turned to water.

"Here?" she asked.

Jax jumped off the walkway and into the muddy water.

"Are you kidding?" asked Cara. "I'm wearing my favorite sandals!"

"Shoulda worn boots, like me," said Jax.

She stood there shaking her head in disbelief. She really didn't want to go with him. The water was dark brown and stagnant looking, about a foot deep over a sludgy bottom.

After a long hesitation, reluctantly, she decided to keep her sandals on—who knew what she might have to step on?—and ducked under the wooden rail, splashing in after him. She felt the cold mud overflow the edges of her shoes and enfold her toes.

"Gross, Jax," she moaned, complaining.

"It's just mud," said Jax, ahead of her.

The water came up higher on him, she realized, but he didn't seem to care. He parted tree branches—it was some kind of thicket, growing right in the water—and they sprang back into her face as she went after him. Plus there were mosquitoes, which were already biting her arms and legs. She slapped at them and shook her head, exasperated.

Jax, of course, was immune to mosquitoes. Or at least, immune to the itching. He never seemed to notice when they bit him.

"You're not even supposed to go off the walkways," she yelled. "If the Park Service sees us, we'll be in trouble."

But Jax was paying no attention.

"It's over here, I think." And he pushed through some wet undergrowth into a shallow hole shaped like a grave and surrounded by twigs and moldy, dead leaves. The hole was lined in what looked like white, chalky pebbles.

"This is a shell midden," said Jax authoritatively.

"A shell what?"

"Midden. It's the remains of human settlement. There are a bunch of them around here, and they can be hundreds of years old, even thousands. This one looks like it's never been excavated; maybe it's even undiscovered. At least, by archaeologists."

"I don't get it, why's there a pile of shells?" she asked impatiently.

"They're mollusk shells, mostly," said Jax. "See? Oysters, mussels…it was probably someone's kitchen midden, and these could be what was left over from their meals. Like a trash pile, more or less."

"So we're supposed to what—go through someone's ancient garbage? To find a finger?"

Jax climbed over the snarl of vegetation and knelt down beside the white depression, his knees on a rotting log.

"Help me," he said.

She sighed, and then she knelt down too.

Combing through the old shells was hard; they were crumbly, and in some places the midden was like a pile of chalk dust. Her fingers turned white with the powder, and when she turned to look at Jax she saw he'd touched his face and left ghostly fingerprints on it.

"Start in this quadrant," said Jax after a minute, pointing to one of the corners. "Move along this way, then begin again here. See? Methodical. That's the key."

"Methodical," she repeated, nodding. "Wow, Jax. This is so fun!"

He kept raking his fingers through the old shells, and after a minute she felt sheepish: he was more patient than she was, and she was supposed to be the mature one. Not sarcastic.

"You're doing a good job, though," she said softly.

He flashed her a quick smile.

It was when Jax smiled that you could tell he was a kid; when he was serious he might as well be a senior citizen.

"Cara! Look!"

It was a row of long, thin shells, splayed out beside each other like—

No. It was a skeleton hand.

"Oh my God," she said. It seemed unreal. She realized she was sweaty and dizzy and let her head fall back so she could stare at the sky. She saw mostly branches.

"Don't worry—Cara! It's not a person, OK? It's not a dead person."

"Not a person?"

She felt dazed.

"Rare to find human remains in a shell midden," said Jax. "No, it looks like a human hand with fingers, but in fact it's a seal flipper. See? Claws."

"Oh," said Cara, letting out her breath.

"It's what she meant," nodded Jax. "Yep. This is it."

"They ate seals? The ancient people?"

"Maybe they were using the blubber for oil. Who knows? Point is, I need to do some mapping."

He pulled out his phone.

"I can pinpoint this using GPS, then use the compass to map a vector from here. It'll give us a general area in the water, at least."

"But which seal finger is it? Look, they're pointing kind of different places. Aren't they?"

"Only one is complete," said Jax. "I'll use that one."

She watched as he knelt down, punching buttons, taking photos with his phone's camera function.

"Do you need my help for this part?" she asked.

"No, take a break," said Jax. "It's cool."

She stood looking through the trees, letting her eyes rest on the water, where insects walked, seeing the movement of tadpoles or minnows now and then. She zoned out. And then, a few minutes later, he was done and packing his equipment back into the knapsack.

"So?" asked Cara. "What did it say?"

"Thing is, I couldn't get quite as precise as I wanted to," said Jax. "My guess would be just offshore at either Nauset or Marconi. But I'm not sure."

"Let's get out of here, then," said Cara. "I'm wet, muddy and covered in mosquito bites."

On their way out, for icing on the cake, she slipped in the water and fell backward, soaking her shorts right through to her underwear. It felt grainy and slimy and made her itch even more than the bugs had. Slogging onward in her wet clothes and clammy sandals—ahead of Jax now in her eagerness to get home and change—she passed under the trees and out into the meadow again, and looked down to see a snake slither right by her foot. She jumped back.

"There are no venomous snakes on the Cape," said Jax. "That was probably a black racer."

"It just startled me," she said, annoyed but resigned. "I'm not afraid of snakes, anyhow."

"I know you're not," said Jax.

"So those middens are—archaeologists come and study them?" she asked.

Jax nodded.

"And that was probably someone's kitchen a long time ago?"

"Not exactly," said Jax. "But close enough. It could have belonged to the Wampanoag, for instance. They lived here for centuries before white people came."

"So now it's ruined, probably. I mean history-wise, we wrecked it. No one will be able to study it now."

"Cara," Jax said gently, "we were the ones who were meant to find it. Think of it that way."

"And the Indians, I mean what if it was sacred to them?"

"It was their *garbage* dump, Cara."

"Still…"

"This isn't just about finding Mom, you know. I mean, obviously."

She stopped walking and looked back at him, startled.

"No?"

"It's bigger than that," said Jax. "Far bigger. You can feel it. I know you can."

She considered for a moment. There was the mysterious and the unexplained—the water falling and falling off the Pouring Man, coming from some unending, invisible source…the ancient turtle hovering just to talk to them, a stream of air rippling and twisting between it and Jax.

Even the skate eggs. Pulsing with some malevolent life.

A secret world hidden in the world they'd always known. A secret all around them.

Yes, she could believe there was something going on.

She could.

But what she wanted was just to find her mother.

"Why us, Jax?" she asked after a while. "I mean, I can see why you would be part of…you're one of a kind. But Max and I—I mean—I'm just an average kid."

Jax reached forward and grabbed her hand.

"Not true," he said.

With his hand in her own she felt better, less like an unpaid assistant to a Great Genius. And for once their two hands, both caked in white, were equally grubby.

There was just enough room on the dirt path for them to walk abreast. Butterflies flitted over the meadow and a mouse darted over the path in front of them. She saw a red-winged blackbird rise out of the tall reeds, and as the two of them cut through the meadow a breeze swept through and swayed all the grass in one direction, with a sound like a long, gentle *hush*.

⚏

They went home, showered (at least Cara did; you never knew with Jax), and changed into dry clothes. Then they each wolfed down a couple of sandwiches, standing up at the kitchen counter. While she was eating, it struck Cara that she'd hardly thought of her mother all day.

Right away she felt guilty, as though she'd betrayed her, as though her mother was being forgotten, and the sandwich turned dry in her mouth.

She wouldn't want me to think of her all the time, she told herself to make herself feel less guilty. *She'd say it wasn't healthy.*

She closed her eyes and pictured her mother smiling as she said that, smiling wryly and shaking her head. It made her feel better, but only a bit.

A few minutes later they got on their bikes again and rode out to meet Max at a mini-golf course where one of his friends had a job. Because Cory worked there they could always play for free, and this way they wouldn't have to worry about their dad hearing them talk about their plans.

When they went in Max was behind the counter helping Cory with customers, which in practice meant handing out scorecards and stubs of pencils and eating stale popcorn from the machine.

He threw back a last handful of popcorn, grabbed three clubs and three different-colored balls, and walked them out onto the first hole, where he put down his ball and teed off into a miniature windmill.

"So? What'd you find out?" asked Jax.

"No luck yet with the Whydahlee," said Max. "I did some research on fires in the ocean, though. It could be vol-

91

canoes, for one. Like submarine volcanoes, right? That's fire under the ocean. Right?"

"Magma, technically," said Jax.

"Problem is, there aren't that many active ones near here. The nearest might be too far for us to get to."

"Like where?" asked Cara.

"Um, the Caribbean," said Max.

"Big help," said Jax.

"Yeah, so I figured that's probably not it," said Max. "So then I figured maybe it's something that hasn't happened yet, you know? Like say a tanker has an oil spill or something, and that catches fire."

"But that wouldn't be under the sea," objected Jax. "It would be on top of it. On the surface."

"True, my man," Max conceded. "I also thought, maybe it's the mid-Atlantic ridge, you know? I guess lava comes up there, from the rift or whatever. But that's a bit of a hike too. Kind of beyond our travel budget."

"Anyway," said Jax, "we know the general area now, and that's not it. It's not going to be too far offshore."

Cara felt disappointed; she'd thought Max would be more help.

"You guys play golf, I'm going to ride down the street," she said. "To buy some fries. Be back in fifteen."

If you cut back down the road behind some buildings there was a greasy spoon/convenience store, one of the mom-and-pop operations off Route 6 that was only open in summer. Their fries were skinny and crunchy. Cara stood in line behind a couple of fishermen, waiting to order; one of them she thought might be Zee's father, a bearded guy who was always sunburnt on his nose, but she wasn't a hundred percent sure.

He was talking to the other guy about work—something about a red tide, which she knew was a bad thing because it meant the shellfishery had to be closed, at least while the red tide lasted. It was bad for business; it hurt the fishermen and in the restaurants it irritated the tourons.

"Chris was saying it's polluted runoff that causes it," said the one who might be Zee's dad.

"No way. It's a natural deal," said the other. "It's algal bloom, man."

At that Cara started and edged closer. Algal bloom… She thought she remembered something about them. They could be phosphorescent, sometimes; they might be poison, but sometimes they were beautiful.

"But pollution can make that stuff happen. They had one in China last month."

She was almost sure it was Zee's dad. Should she ask him? Ask him where the next one was supposed to be?

"You seen one when it's glowing? A few years back there was one like that…glowing all over the bay at night. Friend of mine saw it, I didn't. They didn't shut down the beds that year though."

"In '05 that one came down from Canada, right? But that one didn't glow…. Yeah, hey, Lynn, I'd just like a burger."

"Hi, Lynn, I'll take a burger and a Coke.... Yeah, looks amazing. Kind of this greenish blue on the waves. Those little critters turn bright green, and there are billions of 'em...."

They moved away from the window as Cara stood there, frozen. This was it.

"Just fries, please," she said, distracted.

She had her fries in one hand and was holding her handlebar with the other, bumping slowly back through the gravelly lots behind the row of buildings, when she stopped and whispered it to herself.

"The fires. Green fires beneath the sea."

⸙

"No," said their dad at dinner, which was frozen lasagna since Lolly didn't cook for them on Sundays. "I haven't heard of a red tide this year. Not around here, anyway, or not yet. Why do you ask, Cara?"

"I heard some men talking about it, is all," she said.

"Speaking of men talking," said their dad, "I have to be away tomorrow, and the next night, too. Now, I've been thinking about it, and I can certainly ask Lolly to stay here with you at night, if you'd like. Or one of your old babysitters. But the thing is, most of the ones that are still around are barely older than Max—the older ones have gone off to college. And I was thinking we might try it without a sitter, because I've been impressed lately with your maturity. All three of you, actually. Now, that doesn't mean I wouldn't be nervous. And I'd need you to check in by phone frequently. This would be a first time for us, and it's been a tough summer. But I do know Max is perfectly capable of watching Jax, and Cara, for the most part, can take of herself. Still, if you have any doubt about going it alone, I'd feel better if there was a grownup here with you."

"What are you going away for?" asked Jax.

"I'm supposed to give a paper in Chicago," said their dad. "It was scheduled way back, before…you know. They plan these academic conferences for years in advance. And actually, if any of you don't want me to go—I mean, given the situation, I was thinking of canceling anyway."

"No way," said Max and put down his glass of water. "I can watch Jax. We'll be fine. Really."

"Go," said Cara. "We'll be OK."

"Definitely," said Jax.

"What's the forecast?" asked Cara suddenly.

It had struck her: the three of them alone in the house, at night.

With rain falling.

"I haven't checked," said her dad with a quizzical look. "Why so meteorological?"

"Oh, nothing," she mumbled and stuck her fork into the remains of her lasagna.

Rain again. The rain that brought *him*.

"Lolly will come to make you dinner, anyway," their dad went on. "That much I planned with her already. Both nights, on Monday and Tuesday. But if you're comfortable with Max as a babysitter, she'll just go home after that."

"I promise," said Max and raised his hands like he was surrendering. "No wild parties."

"And no girls over," said their dad, and then coughed discreetly.

Usually he didn't even go there; it was their mother's job to have the embarrassing conversations with them about safe sex and responsibility. She'd just had one with Cara this spring. Even though she was pretty easy to talk to, it still made Cara cringe to think about it. Ugh. Why did they even bother?

"Scout's honor," said Max, nodding.

Jax had pulled out his phone and was typing away on it. His fingers were small, and he could go incredibly fast, even over the miniscule buttons. Cara could tell he was on the Web; the house had wireless. Then he put it away again.

"The forecast," he told them, "is for storms."

Five

"See, the bioluminescence associated with some red tides, or algal blooms," said Jax to Cara the next morning, while they were out walking Rufus, "is caused by phytoplankton."

They'd waved their dad off to catch the boat for Boston; Max had gone with him on the twenty-minute drive to the ferry dock and would bring the car back. Then they'd headed out on their morning dogwalk, toward the general store that was beside the small post office. The store carried donuts sometimes, which were baked fresh at the beginning of the day. Jax had a thing for their bear claws.

"...basically, a whole bunch of microorganisms thrown together," said Jax, in lecture mode. "And the phytoplankton that make up these kind of blooms are often dinoflagellates. One species in particular has been noted for its bioluminescence: *Lingulodinium polyedrum.*"

Dino-whatever-it-was rang a bell—she'd heard the word recently. Maybe at her mother's office—Roger talking about her mother's research. Which meant this obscure—algae?— had cropped up twice in just a couple of days. That seemed like a strange coincidence.

"So, once we know where to look," said Jax, "that's what we'll be looking for. A kind of light on the waves."

"You think that's really it? The fires beneath the sea?"

"I do," said Jax. "You saw it, Cara. You really did."

She felt a small surge of satisfaction.

"You know," she said slowly, as they waited to cross Route 6, "I didn't tell you what I heard Dad and Roger talking about when I went into Mom's office."

"What?" said Jax quickly.

She saw his look and winced. *That* was why she hadn't told him—he was ten, and he missed their mother, and maybe, just maybe, their mother was missing because she'd been...what had their dad said?

Taken.

But she should have told him before. She had to tell him things, even if he was young—even if, sometimes, he looked into her brain when he wasn't supposed to.

"There was a break-in at her office," she said haltingly. She found she was still pretty reluctant to talk about it. "And Roger, you know, her boss?—he was telling Dad that they stole her work off her computer."

"*Stole* it?" asked Jax.

"The data, he said? Or dataset, something like that."

The light had changed, but Jax was just standing still, holding onto Rufus's leash, looking up at her.

"They took her data?" he asked.

Cara nodded. She felt guilty: she really should have told him, and Max, too.

There was just something about all of them, at the moment, that had made her not want to say it out loud...life in their house seemed so delicately balanced lately, as though—even before the Pouring Man—things were barely holding together, a kind of imitation of their old life. They kept to the same routine, her dad doing his research, Max working his job at the restaurant and hanging out at the courts or the skatepark, Jax trekking off to daycamp or doing his databases...but through it all they were just going through the motions.

And waiting.

They were on hold until real life began again.

Her mother *was* real life, she thought.

Also, if you didn't let yourself talk about something, it stayed a little unreal. It stayed an arm's length away. Once it was mentioned, there was a kind of concreteness to it.

"This was the numbers on ocean pH and shellfish?" prodded Jax.

"I don't—it kind of went over my head. They said 'CO_2' a lot, but that's all I know."

"Dad was talking to me about that project on the drive home that day," said Jax, nodding as he made the connection. "But he didn't say anything about information theft or hackers...."

"Let's go," said Cara, because the light was blinking DON'T WALK already.

"I'm tired of being treated like an infant," said Jax suddenly, more loudly than usual. "I don't deserve it. Why didn't he tell me? Why didn't *you*?"

She looked at him, then at the DON'T WALK sign again. Jax wasn't budging.

The sign froze, and cars started speeding by them again.

"I guess—"

"What? You have to tell me *everything*. We're in this together!"

"Then you have to *promise* not to ping me again without asking. Ever," she said, with a loudness that matched his own. "Or else I can't trust you, either!"

They looked at each other.

"OK," said Jax, more quietly. "I promise if you do. I'll always ask before I read you."

"And I'll tell you what I know," she said.

They stood there for another minute, waiting for the light to change back, and finally crossed, a little awkward, with Rufus loping beside them.

"She was supposed to go to Washington and tell Congress what her study said," she added when they reached the opposite sidewalk. "Maybe so they could pass a new law about it or something? And then…" She trailed off. "And then she disappeared, Jaxy."

"But ocean acidification is common knowledge," said Jax. "At least, in the scientific community. I mean, it's not like she's cornered the market on marine pH dropping. Lots of people are studying it."

There was the general store, with a bakery beside it and the small post office. A few feet behind the row of shops, past a thin screen of trees, the bike path ran almost the whole length of the Outer Cape—along the edge of the strip of forest that gave way to cliffs and dune grass and sand, and then the surging Atlantic.

She wished she could just ride again, the way she used to—coast along the smooth path, warmed by the sun.... It was what she'd always loved to do, every summer since she first started taking off by herself. She coasted with her hands free, the seashore on her right with its pine and oak-tree woods, creeks with frogs splashing and silver fish flashing through them, marshes with herons, ponds with water lilies. There were the soft-looking deer that ambled through the patchwork shade of the trees, where the old dirt roads wound through the cool forest and came out on the bright cliffs in the sun with their wild roses trembling as the breeze swept over them...on her left side were the distant sounds of a steady river of traffic, the long row of shabby, cozy motels on Route 6. There were the seafood restaurants with their ocean themes, round windows like portholes, and old rusty-orange life preservers hanging in nets on the walls.

And where there weren't restaurants there were the friendly neighborhoods where kids played, their wind-worn saltbox houses covered in climbing roses, and behind them, next to the path, the rambling, overgrown green backyards....

The Cape, they taught in school, was just a big sand bar beneath their feet; it was young, in geological terms, only a few thousand years old, made of the silt left behind by glaciers. It would be gone soon, they said, like a pile of dirt in a puddle of rainwater—going, going, gone....

But she was here now. She wasn't going anywhere.

And she wished so much she could be sure, the way she used to be, that when she decided to go home again both her parents would be there waiting.

The feeling—which was almost like longing, or like a caught sob that didn't go away—faded a bit as they went into the general store, stopping to tie up Rufus outside. It was one of their old haunts, being so near their house. She liked its dusty wooden floors, its dimly lit, homey atmosphere. When they were younger, and allowed to walk to the store by themselves for the first time, their dad used to let them pick up the newspaper for him. He would give them a couple of dollars extra to get snacks for themselves, along with the paper for him, two coffees, and a bagel with cream cheese for their mother.

Jax beat her over to the fresh baked-goods section, where they had muffins and donuts if you got there early enough.

"No bear claws," said Jax glumly.

"Have the raised maple," she said.

"Maple," said Jax and made a face. "Who eats that? It's so weird. Plus it's the color of vomit."

Max honked the horn at them in a jaunty rhythm as they were walking home, pulling up alongside. *Duh-duh-duh-duh-duh, duh duh.* Her dad always sang to that rhythm, some old-time jingle: "Shave-and-a-haircut, two bits."

"I got it!" Max called out as the passenger window rolled down so that they could hear him.

They stood there for a second with Rufus on the side-walk, and then Cara bent down to look through the window.

"Got what?" she asked.

"The *Whydah!* It wasn't the Whydahlee or Whydah Lee, it was just the *Whydah!* Get it? The *lee side* of the *Whydah!*"

"What's the *Whydah?*"

"A pirate ship!"

Max was exuberant—obviously happy he'd redeemed himself by solving the mystery.

"A pirate ship?"

"It's sunk right off Marconi! It wrecked there in 1717. I saw stuff about it in P-town, where they have that pirate museum. I was dropping Dad off, you know? And we ended up having to park in the lot near the pier, and then he got on the boat, and I was walking back to the car and I saw the pirate flag and went in. It's right there on the pier. And inside there was this whole thing on how they've dug up artifacts from the *Whydah,* and where it is, and everything!"

"C'mon, Jax," said Cara, "let's just get in." And she opened the car door for Rufus, who leapt past them.

As they pulled away from the curb Max was still bab-bling excitedly.

"It's this pirate's ship that's, like, less than a mile off the beach. Totally underwater. It's not that far out at all. I figure I can get Zee to bring out her dad's powerboat, you know?

She's great with it, she can totally handle the steering. And we can use their scuba gear, or maybe Cory's. They have it all, the tanks, everything. Even wet suits. I think there's even a buoy out where the *Whydah* is, you know? Because this treasure-hunter guy has, like, an exclusive on it, it's some kind of finders, keepers deal? He found the wreck back in the eighties and ever since then he's been pulling stuff out of it, artifacts and things. Swords and pistols and jewelry...."

"A real, actual pirate ship," said Cara. "I didn't know there were any of those around."

"Hardly any," said Max. "Just the *Whydah,* as far as I could find out. On the Cape, anyway. And it's three centuries old. It's pronounced like *widow*, by the way. Or *widda*, or something. That's what it means, it's some old-fashioned spelling. And most of it you can't see even if you're diving. Most of it's under the sand. They use this fancy vacuum to suck up all the pieces of the boat. And the treasure."

"We still don't know *when* to go, though," said Jax. "Even if we can be sure where."

"Listen, if we really mean it," said Max, "there's only one way to do it. We have to patrol. We'll have to do it in shifts, trade off sleeping. Have someone out there every night, watching for your glow-in-the-dark waterbugs, or whatever they are."

"They're not *bugs* at all," said Jax. "They're *dinoflagellates.*"

Cara was thinking that Max's newfound enthusiasm was almost funny. Just give a guy a pirate ship...

"I'm thinking we each take a friend, then switch off. Like Cara? You could go with Hayley say from nine to one in the morning, then I could go over with my crew. Jax, though—being only ten and all?—maybe should stay at home."

"Unfair," said Jax. "Age discrimination, apartheid, and segregation."

"You heard what dad said," said Max. "I'm the boss."

They were silent for a minute, Jax sulking.

"Whoever saw them, obviously," put in Cara, "would call the others right away on the cell. 'Cause we all have to be there for the actual dive. Ultimately. So Jax, all you'll miss is the boring part. Are you kidding? You're *lucky*."

They talked about it as they pulled up to the house and got out, walking up the front steps. Max suggested they reveal only part of the story to their friends—tell them they were looking for the luminous algae, but say they had to do it for Jax, who had been assigned a big science project for a gifted-kids think tank in Washington, DC. (It was true that a school for geniuses there wanted him. It was even true that he was working on a project for them—or at least he had been. But their mother had been his advisor on the project, and it was kind of in limbo, since she wasn't around.)

Cara wanted to tell Hayley the truth. She felt bad about hiding it from her. She'd been keeping a lot to herself lately. And even if Hayley hadn't believed her about the driftwood thing…Hayley was her friend, and it felt awkward to keep this a secret. But Max said it was all too much; he said the bizarreness of the story would stress out their friends.

"I mean, let's face it," said Max. "Who would believe the story about the turtle mind meld? It adds this whole other level of weirdness and explaining. Plus, let me be frank, I don't want to be seen as a freak. Let's take the path of least resistance. Feel me?"

He planned to tell Zee and his other friends that the scuba-diving trip was to collect algae for Jax, for him to study it, but that the whole thing had to be secret from Zee's father. After all, you weren't really supposed to swim in red tides, and her father probably wouldn't let them.

"Plus I still have to figure out how to teach you guys scuba at warp speed," added Max. "And right now? I don't have clue one."

❧

Cara stopped by Hayley's house to invite her to sleep over.

"I'll go ask," said Hayley, and left Cara standing in the front hallway looking at her mom's big shelf of figurines, which she liked to show off whenever she got a new one on ebay. They were called Hummers, or something. They made Cara feel ill. There was a chubby girl with a white goose, a gnome with a basket of mushrooms, a drummer boy with a flag on his shoulder.... Cara thought they were sort of ugly, but they had big, round eyes and pink cheeks, and Hayley's mom loved whatever she thought was cute.

Once Cara's own mother had stood here with her—they had come in to talk about carpooling or something—and Cara had seen her look at the statuettes with kind eyes. She smiled reassuringly at Cara as they waited, then looked at the figurines again, studiously, examining them—not like they were cute but like they were very, very strange. Cara's mother had a way of looking at tacky stuff sometimes that was kind of deliberate and quizzical—like she was a traveler from afar, born in a different, finer place, where such things did not exist.

Although apparently she was born in Topeka. Where they probably had plenty of Hummers of their own.

Actually, come to think of it, Cara wasn't sure where her mother had been born, though for some reason she had a vague picture of cornfields with windmills slowly, creakily turning, or maybe the black-and-white landscape Dorothy lived in before she went to Oz. Her mother didn't talk much about her childhood.

Cara heard Hayley ask her mother if she could stay over at Cara's house. Her mother seemed to be scrubbing the bathtub, to judge by the back-and-forth scratching that went on and on as Hayley talked, so Hayley must be standing outside the bathroom door.

Her mother had kind of a carrying voice.

"I guess so, honey," said her mother.

Hayley mumbled something about Cara's dad not being there to supervise.

"Well, that family needs a *lot of extra support*," said her mother, who sounded like she was trying to be discreet but was actually practically yelling. Cara cringed. "We have to be real supportive of *that whole family*."

Anyway, said Hayley's mother, they were right down the street, so as long as Hayley called her if anything made her uncomfortable…

Out on the sidewalk, while Hayley tossed a tennis ball up and down and popped her gum, Cara explained that she had a science project of Jax's to help with, and would Hayley mind spending a few hours on the beach that night?

Then they would come back here. Hayley could borrow Max's bike, since she didn't have a light on her own.

Hayley shook her head uncertainly. She didn't like to keep things from her mom; it was just the two of them.

"Max is pitching a tent for us," Cara added. "We'll trade off shifts. So he'll be there, too—you know, part of the time."

Which she had to admit was sort of devious of her, since she knew Hayley had a big crush on Max.

But this was about getting their mother back. Desperate measures…

"Oh," said Hayley and nodded. "OK, then."

⊰⊱

They went to a pool that belonged to one of Max's friends, whose parents were off at work, and practiced with the scuba gear for a couple of hours, mostly in the deep end. It made Cara nervous, but Jax liked dealing with the equipment; he was always a quick study. The tanks were surprisingly heavy, she thought, and you had to trust that other people knew how to fill them off a big machine and then

108

carefully check them—Max, in this case. Who had been diving with Cory for years but still didn't have his certification.

Then they spent the rest of the afternoon getting ready for beach camping, which Jax solemnly informed them was against the law. Or at least Park Service rules. They'd have to be stealthy and sneak down after dark, and just hope that no rangers would come driving along the beach in their Park Service jeeps to notice them.

The gear needed to be ready and stowed in their big, external-frame backpacks before Lolly got there to make dinner so there was no chance of her noticing anything.

"Why don't we set the tent up under the trees on the cliffs, overlooking the beach?" suggested Cara. "Not far from the parking lot, so it's easy to get to in the dark. And it's not right at the water, in fact it's a long way up, so that makes it harder for him to get to us."

The three of them were in the garage digging up camping gear from previous years, when the family had made road trips out West to hike in the red-rock country of Utah and near the Grand Canyon. Cara remembered her mother laughing as the wind tossed one of their picnics into the air—running, as she held Cara's hand, through a high alpine meadow where there were purple lupines....

This summer, of course, there'd been no road trips.

"From up on the bluffs we'll definitely have a view of the water," she pressed. "A *better* view. We can see way further out from up there. So if the glow's all the way out at

the shipwreck, say?—and doesn't come up to the waterline, we'll still be able to spot it. And there'll be less chance
anyone will catch us."

Human or otherwise, she thought.

Max was rolling up sleeping bags and pads and stow-
ing them in the back of the car. He thought they should take
those along in case their friends got bored and wanted to
crash; the four-person tent had a clear-mesh door flap, so the
others could just lie down while Cara or Max kept a lookout.

"You're probably right," he said. "Plus, if we hit paydirt,
and we have to call Zee to bring the boat out, we get better
cell coverage up there, too."

"'Course the downside," said Jax, "is you'll have more
mosquitoes."

"Note to self: pack bug juice," said Max.

The garage was dusty, with cobwebs clinging to the
boxes of battery-powered lanterns and lightweight cooking
equipment. Cara brushed them off and wiped her hands on
her jeans.

"So, here's how we'll do it," said Max. "I'll drive over
early and pitch the tent, OK? I'll leave the bags and pads in
there, flashlights and lantern, drinks, insect repellent"—he
looked down at the pile of gear, nodding as he took stock of
what they'd need—"and some snacks. Also extra batteries
for the lantern, cause we wouldn't want to run out of light.
After I set it all up, I come back and we all have dinner with
Lolly and act like normal kids."

"Act like," said Cara.

"Then, as soon as Lolly goes home, you and Hayley take off on the bikes. Me and the guys'll come relieve you at one in the morning, in the car. We'll do the rest of the night shift. It's no problem. Keat wants to play poker with nickels. But we all gotta sync up our watches. And charge our phones."

"I'll man the home base," said Jax. "Even if I can't go with you, I can still stay up and help. You're not giving me a curfew now, are you Max?"

"No curfew, little dude."

"So you can text me any questions. And report back hourly, just to check in."

"Especially if it's raining," said Cara. "Because if it rains...."

"Exactly. Is this thing waterproof?" asked Jax, and lifted a corner of their family's old red tent.

"Used to be," said Max. "Not so sure anymore. But it's not like we're camping out for days on end or anything."

"I mean, because of him," said Jax. "Night and rain. Those are his favorite things."

"His?" asked Max.

"Pouring man," said Jax.

"The man who walks in water," Cara said with a nod.

"As opposed to *on* water," added Jax.

"Wait. On water, as in Jesus?" asked Max.

"*In* water," said Jax.

"He sure isn't Jesus," said Cara. "Way too creepy."

Jax shook his head. "And no beard."

But a slow, steady drizzle began after Max drove off to pitch the tent, telling Lolly he had to pick up his paycheck at the restaurant.

"Great," whispered Cara to Jax, helping to set the table. "Rain, like you forecasted."

"I still wish I was going with you," said Jax.

"Going where, dear?" asked Lolly, bustling in with a basket of bread.

"To-to-to...," he stammered.

"To school with me in the fall," broke in Cara, grabbing at straws. "See, they were going to skip him ahead some grades, but Mom and Dad said he was 'developmentally inappropriate' for my grade. He's kind of disappointed."

"Oh, dear," said Lolly and patted Jax's head as though he were Rufus. "Don't be in such a hurry to grow up. It's more fun being a kid."

"Yeah, right," said Jax.

After she went back into the kitchen they stood staring over the table at the windows beyond, a stack of place mats and napkins in front of them. Cara could see through the trees in their backyard to the rain falling over the bay, freshwater joining the salt ocean in a million minuscule pinpricks on the surface. Soon you wouldn't be able to see out there at all; already dusk was coming on, and with all the dark clouds overhead it seemed even later.

The branches of the pines dipped and swayed, and beyond them the gray of water and sky seemed to combine without a line between them, into a vague mist.

"Is that what they really said?" he asked after a minute. "I'm not mature enough?"

Cara looked at his hurt face and was surprised, then felt a pang of shame that she hadn't thought of his feelings.

"I was just making it up, mostly," she said.

This was one of those times she needed him to keep his promise—his promise not to ping her.

"I mean," she said, scratching a bite on her arm to give the impression she wasn't focused on fibbing, "they did think you should be with kids your own age, though. They said you'd have no fun if you were with thirteen-year-olds. That it would be too weird."

"But I get along with you," he said. "You're thirteen."

"Come on, Jax," she said gently. "That's different. *You* know what I mean."

He shrugged defensively and turned back to the window.

"I don't know," she said hesitantly. She didn't want to make him as nervous as she was about tonight, but she felt so unsure.… They had no idea what they were doing, after all. It was a giant shot in the dark. They were trusting that all this *meant* something. That it was real—not just a figment of her and Jax's imagination, which it sometimes seemed to be—and that the signs they were finding were meant for *them*. "We're going to be out there at night, with the rain and the lightning, and we're taking the others, Hayley and Keat and Cory or whoever, without telling them what we're there to do—maybe putting them in danger, even. And we don't even know why, exactly.…"

"We *do* know," said Jax firmly. "We're doing it for her. And not only that, either. We know there's something bigger. We know there's a pattern behind it. We just don't quite see what the pattern is. Not yet. But we *are* supposed to do this, Car. We've been spoken to—you with the letters on the driftwood, the message from the sea. Me with the sea turtle."

"And don't forget *him*," said Cara, picking up a napkin ring and twisting the yellow cotton napkin inside it.

"No," said Jax, and shook his head. "How could I? He spoke to us too. There are two sides to this fight, and we've been approached by both of them."

"That message," said Cara, laying forks around the places. "It said 'three,' which you think means us, and then called those three the 'interpreter, arbiter and visionary.' Right? Well, I can see how you'd be the visionary. But Max and I don't exactly seem like interpreters or judges. That's what arbiter means, right?"

"One who weighs both sides," said Jax, nodding. "An impartial decision-maker, in this case."

"So how *can* it be us, then?"

"Just be patient," said Jax. "Don't think you have to understand everything at once. Sometimes it takes a while. You have to wait and see. You have to believe it'll be clear one day, as long as you keep watching."

⊰⊱

After dinner they were impatient for Lolly to leave, but she seemed to think it was her job to clear and wash every last dish and then tuck the kids in—despite the fact that Max didn't typically go to bed till midnight even on school nights.

So all four of them, including Hayley, pretended to be tired, yawning and rubbing their eyes sleepily. By 8:30 Lolly apparently believed they were down for the count. She set the dishwasher churning and sloshing, turned out all the lights downstairs, and called up her good-nights to each of them before she headed out the front door toward her car, running with a magazine held over her head to keep dry, and drove off up the street.

They watched from Max's window to be sure she was safely gone.

"You're lucky," said Hayley enviously. "I wouldn't be left alone ever. My mom won't even let me walk to the store by myself. She says stuff like 'ten thousand children are abducted in this country.'"

"You're what, fourteen, and she doesn't let you walk to the store?" asked Max.

He was wearing a faded T-shirt that said KNOW YOUR RIGHTS; apparently his right was to pick his ear, which he was rooting around in with a pinky.

Cara was grossed out, but Hayley didn't look any less lovestruck. Cara couldn't help pulling a face.

"She's thirteen, like me," she said.

"Fourteen really soon, though," put in Hayley.

115

"What's she gonna do, hide in your closet when you go to college?"

"I *know*, right?" said Hayley. "It's embarrassing."

"Come on, Hay, we should go," said Cara, and tugged her friend's arm to get her away from Max, a/k/a the Ear-picking Heartthrob. "It's already dark. We could be missing it."

"You got a really great brother and sister here," said Hayley to Jax as they went out Max's door. Mostly to kiss up to Max, obviously. "All this for a science project!"

Hayley wasn't used to riding a bike at night, so Cara took the lead and went slowly. They crossed Route 6 with no headlights in sight, only the rain pattering down on the hoods of their jackets and the tires making soft *whishing* sounds over the wet pavement. When they got to the Marconi parking lot, they walked their bikes up out of the lot and onto the cliffside, taking a narrow, bumpy trail over the bluffs to where the tent was pitched, hidden by low pines.

And sure enough, Cara found the tent in the dark by hearing instead of sight: the drops hitting its sides made a sound that was different from the rain on the trees and the sandy grass.

While Hayley laid Max's bike down and scrambled to get inside and get dry, Cara stood for a minute looking out over the ocean. It was invisible—a huge, black abyss. Her eyes would adjust, she figured, if they didn't turn the lantern on inside the tent; but if they kept a light on the whole time, she'd definitely have trouble seeing what she was supposed to be here to see.

She followed Hayley into the tent, where blankets were piled on top of the sleeping bags. Hayley flicked a flashlight on, and Cara realized she wouldn't be able to see anything from inside anyway—it was impossible to know whether, looking out the mesh of the door flap, she was seeing the black sky or the black sea. She could easily miss whatever phosphorescence appeared in the water, and she wouldn't even know she wasn't looking in the right place.

But the tent was safer. From him.

The tent was dry and well lit.

Still, if she stayed safe inside the tent she really could miss seeing the fires. Then she would fail the test.

And she couldn't stand that. Because finally, she realized, it was a test of whether she cared enough, and was strong enough, to bring her mother back.

At least, if the Pouring Man came, she could hide from him in the tent. It was dry, after all, and he couldn't come in unless she let him, Jax had said.

"I have to stand outside, I think," she told Hayley. "But you can bundle up and keep warm, right? There's snacks somewhere in here, too. Max left them."

"You're going to stand out in the rain?" asked Hayley.

"Sorry. But I have to," said Cara.

Hayley shook her head. "I may be an only child and all? But if I did have a brother, I'm really not sure I would go through all this just so he could, like, look at slimy bugs through a microscope."

"They're not exactly bugs," said Cara. "They're dinoflagellates. Phytoplankton that are bioluminescent."

She could hardly believe she'd got all the syllables in the right order. She felt almost as smart as Jax.

"Whatev," said Hayley.

Cara moved away from the tent and stood under one of the taller pines. The longer she stood still, staring out to a sea that didn't even seem to be there, the more she wished she had a folding chair.

Huddled with her cell phone sheltered inside her raised jacket collar—and partly to distract herself from her nervousness—she dialed Jax.

"Tell Max you can't see anything from inside the tent," she said. "He needs to bring a lawn chair or something for the person who's keeping watch. Even though it's raining. So, Max'll have to watch for *him* the whole time, too. He'll have to watch the sea and watch for the Pouring Man. And even if he's going to end up getting soaked, he probably still won't want to just have to stand out here for five hours."

She finally found a tree branch to sit on, a short way along the edge of the cliff. To her left was the red glow of the lantern from inside the tent, as Hayley read a magazine about celebrities—her main provision for the evening, which she'd brought a whole stack of. To Cara's right there were no lights at all unless she looked out to sea, where a cruise ship was sitting with its swooping strings of yellow-white lights like Christmas decorations.

No lights nearby. Except the tent's lantern.

Her fingers were getting cold, slick with rainwater where they stuck out of the end of her sleeves. She tried hopping from one foot to another to keep her toes warm, realizing she should have worn thick wool socks instead of thin ones beneath her Pumas. It was surprisingly cold for August, standing out here at night with the light rain falling. She listened to the waves crash below and the drizzle patter down on the leaves around her and thought of her mother. The lines in the message—the poem that supposedly told them what they needed to do—her mother had to have left that in the shell box for them, right? Because who else could have gone in and put it there? So, did that mean her mother was the one who had scratched the message on driftwood, too?

It was a strange thought, the idea that her mother might possibly have been watching her—watching her and Rufus on their morning walk, making their way down the sand road a short time after dawn, and never showed herself.

And when had her mother had a chance to put the message in the mother-of-pearl box—just a few days ago? Weeks? If she'd put it there recently, as in this summer— if she could come and go as she liked—why hadn't she let them know she was safe? And why communicate in complicated language instead of just saying right out what they were supposed to do?

119

She felt a surge of resentment. First her mother had left them without warning, now she was making them do hard things—jump through these crazy hoops without even explaining why.

At least, Cara hoped it was her. Because if it was someone else, that was scarier still.

She thought she heard a faint rustle in the trees behind her. Was it him?

She tensed, ready to dash back into the tent. Then she looked to her left and noticed there was no red light emanating from the tent anymore. It was dark all around her. She should have told Hayley to keep the light on, she should have made that clear! She could take a break, couldn't she? Five minutes. The red tide couldn't come and go *that* quickly.

She had to get the light on again. She had to be able to see.

She edged toward the tent, not wanting to use her flashlight, and felt panicky when, kneeling down in front of the opening, she fumbled with the zipper on the door and couldn't get it to unzip—a panic as though there was something right there at her back, something unknown bending down....

Then the zipper gave, and she slipped inside, her heart beating fast.

Hands shaking, she zipped it up again.

"Hey, Car," came Hayley's tired voice beside her in the dark as she turned over and her sleeping bag made its swishing sound. "Did you find any of those dinoflatulence?"

"Not yet," said Cara, and flicked the lantern on. "Sorry, but we really need to keep the light on. We *have* to."

"Mmm," murmured Hayley, not caring.

Cara pulled a blanket around herself to warm up, her teeth chattering.

Hayley's breathing got slow and regular again—she'd fallen back to sleep. Cara told herself she could relax briefly, too—she could lie back for just five minutes, couldn't she? Before she went outside again. Just five minutes.

⚓

In the dream, her mother was in the tent with her. Cara could almost smell her clean, lemony skin, a saltiness in her long, dark hair.

"Cara," sighed her mother. "Cara. Cara."

Her hair was flowing like a mermaid's. Was that soft water around them? Or just the plain old air?

"Come *home*," said Cara, begging. "Where are you?"

"Nearby, sweetie," breathed her mother. Her voice was warm and comforting.

"Why aren't you home with us?" asked Cara plaintively. She wanted to reach out for her mother, but her arms were not moving. She couldn't get them to rise no matter how much she wanted them to. They weighed nothing, as though they were not attached to her.

"I'm in hiding," whispered her mother. "Not from you, honey. But I can't let you know where, exactly. If you knew where I was, then he would, too. He's like Jax, in that way."

"The Pouring Man?" Cara asked.

"His name is fear," came her mother's voice softly.

"What does he want with you?" asked Cara.

"He's one of the soldiers of the Cold One," murmured her mother. "The Cold One's army of dead soldiers…"

"His dead what—? What do you mean?"

"Long, long story," said her mother, and she seemed to be fading. Her voice came like a wave now, or the wind, with a kind of whisper. "But you are *needed*, Cara. All three of you are. In the struggle against them. And he doesn't want us to be together for the struggle, because we're weaker if he can keep us apart. He wants to keep you away from me, and keep you away from the others, too."

"The other who?"

"Others like me," said her mother and swirled in midair, getting blurry. For a second Cara thought she was floating on her back. Her voice was getting almost too thin and soft to hear. "Others among the guardians."

"Why can't you just tell us what to *do*, then?" Cara cried out, impatient.

"The more you know, the more easily he can know too," said her mother, but now she was almost gone, getting smaller and farther away. She was receding. But Cara didn't want her to.

"Don't go," said Cara. "It's too hard! I can't find you!"

"You will," said her mother. "You'll see. Because it's you, Cara. *You* are the visionary."

And Cara sat bolt upright in the dark.

She was breathing hard. She tried to calm herself, counting to ten until her breath came more evenly.

"Hayley?" she asked finally.

No answer. Hayley wasn't in the tent at all.

She must have needed to go to the bathroom, Cara thought—there were bathrooms at the edge of the parking lot, along with the outdoor showers.

And Cara hadn't told her about the danger. Cara hadn't told her anything, and now she might be out there with *him*.

Rain was still pattering down on the tent; she would wait another minute or two and then go find her friend. The dream had seemed so real, except for the way her mother hung suspended in front of her.... But how could *she* be the visionary? Jax was the one who seemed to know everything, who had special powers....

She heard a hand on the door flap, scrabbling at it—trying to open the zipper in the dark. Hayley, come back. It was a relief. She groped for the lantern to help unzip the flap, and after a minute had the light switched on, illuminating Hayley's fingers.

"Here," she said. "That better?"

But Hayley's fingers couldn't get it to work—it was a sticky zipper—so Cara reached out and undid it herself.

"There, I got it finally," she said. "Come in!"

Hayley kneeled and came through—the top of her head first, with its straggly part and light-blond hair. When she was all the way in, past Cara and settling down to sit on her own sleeping bag, she raised her face.

And Cara saw there was water running off her. Out of her wide-open eyes. Down her cheeks and her neck. Pouring.

And at the same time she thought: *I asked her to come in.*

Cara screamed. She couldn't help it.

Before she even registered what she was doing she had thrown herself past not-Hayley, out the unzipped door flap, and was sprinting in a blind terror for the parking lot— toward wherever there might be light, the signs of civilization.

She ran pell-mell toward the parking lot and the cement-block restroom building, her feet slipping and sliding on the muddy trail, bumping into wet branches and slick grass as she went—

A light went on in the dark. It was the light outside the women's room, on the wall of the building. It must have been triggered by motion, must go on whenever someone came near…and then she was inside the women's room, which she'd never thought she'd be so glad to get to.

Something had stung her cheek, and she put her fingers up reflexively. They came away with blood on them. A cut from a pine branch, probably.

The bathroom was the same as ever. Fluorescent tubes overhead shone down on sinks and toilet stalls and the grubby gray tile floor.

And in front of the blurry mirrors stood Hayley.

Again.

Cara felt another scream rising but stifled it, stumbling back with her hands out, grasping for the walls and the door; at the same time, Hayley turned and gaped at her. She looked pretty much like she always did—no water pouring, none at all. Her face was dry and familiar. She was chewing her usual strawberry-flavored gum, which Cara could smell, and wore too much blue eyeliner.

It was light in here, after all. Light and dry.

"Is it you?" blurted Cara. "Hayley! Is it you?"

"Um," said Hayley, "who else would it be? What is *up* with you? What happened to your face, girl?"

"He made himself look just like you," said Cara, breathing raggedly, shaking her head.

She leaned over, bracing her hands on her thighs while she caught her breath. She couldn't believe it. It was impossible. Water was one thing, but this?

Then she remembered something Jax had told her: something like eighty percent of the human body was water.

Was that how he managed it? Being the master of water?

And she had invited him in. She'd said *Come in*, believing it was Hayley. He had tricked her.

Would he follow them here?

She turned around and looked closely at the door, trying to find a lock. Hayley was saying something, but Cara was too frantic to pay attention to her. The lock wasn't the right kind, though—the door could only be locked from the outside, for one thing, and to do that you would need a key. So she backed up against it, just in case. Trying to hold it closed with her weight.

"*Cara!* He who?" repeated Hayley.

Of course. Hayley thought they were doing a science project, and now Cara had blown it. But who cared about the details—he was close. He could get them any minute. It was still raining.

"We can't go back to the tent," she said.

Her mind was racing. She didn't know what he could do to them. What had her mother said? He wanted to come between them; he didn't want them to find her. *His name was fear*, and he wanted to keep them apart....

And even if he was gone from the tent by now, he might have left some of his water there. Right? She couldn't forget how carefully Jax had lifted that towel—how deliberate and grim he had seemed. You couldn't touch where the Pouring Man had been. You couldn't take that risk.

His name is fear, her mother had said. *He is a dead soldier.*

Who knew what that was supposed to mean? A dead soldier? It made her feel kind of sorry for him, if he was a soldier who had died. But then the Pouring Man wasn't someone she thought she could feel sorry for.

It made no sense.

"Why not?" asked Hayley.

"We just can't," said Cara. "Trust me."

Her back still against the thick metal door, she fumbled in her pocket and pulled out her cell.

"Max," she said when he answered. "Help. He's here. Come pick us up in the parking lot, beside the bathroom building. And come now!"

She clicked the phone shut to find Hayley staring at her, so amazed she was even forgetting to chew her gum.

"What's going on?" asked Hayley. "Come on. Tell me!"

"It's, it's just this guy," said Cara. "He's been hanging around the house lately. We don't like him. And now he's followed me here."

"What, like a molester dude?" asked Hayley.

"Not exactly," said Cara.

"Because if it's a Peeping Tom or something, my mom is gonna *freak*," said Hayley, turning back to the sinks to wash her hands. "There was this guy across the street last spring? Renting the Klosterman house? And he—"

Cara couldn't listen. Her stomach was still flipping. He could be close; he could be right outside. The windows of the bathroom were frosted so you couldn't see out, and threaded through with squares of wire. As windows they were completely useless.

"Here, lean against the door with me," she told Hayley. "Just in case he tries to get in."

She didn't know what the rules were when the place was public—maybe here he didn't have to be invited. Maybe here he was free to come and go as he pleased.

"But how'll we know when it's Max?"

"We'll hear him," said Cara. "And the car, we'll hear it pull up. *He* doesn't drive a car. He's always…walking."

"He, like the perv?"

"He's not—whatever. Yeah. Basically, him."

Both of them were lined up against the door beside each other now, their backs to it, their arms down at their sides. It took eight minutes to get here from their house—she knew that by heart, since she and Max been coming to Marconi since she was tiny—and more if there was traffic.

She looked at her watch; Max should be here in five minutes now. Could they hold him off for that long?

"So, when did this guy start bugging you?" Hayley was asking, sounding kind of urgent. Cara wanted to tell her to be quiet, but she didn't want to seem mean. She'd brought Hayley here; she was the one putting her friend in danger....

"You left the faucet on," Cara noticed.

"Oh. Whoops," said Hayley, and darted forward to turn it off.

"No, no, stay put!" cried Cara. "I need your weight on the door. He's stronger than me. He's stronger than both of us!"

"Aright, aright, chillax," said Hayley, already back at the door.

Cara felt a small surge of relief.

"Can't hear the rain," said Hayley. "Can you?"

"That'd be good, if it stopped raining," said Cara, and tried to listen. But the walls of the restroom were pretty thick and it was hard to tell.

Her watch said two minutes more.

"Shoot," said Hayley. "That faucet must be broken."

The tap was on again.

"The plumbing in this place never did work that well," said Cara. "Just leave it this time, 'K? I need you here, against the door."

And then she looked harder at the stream of water coming from the tap.

Water. Of course.

She felt stupid. And then she also felt afraid.

Steam was rising from the water column, as though it was boiling. The steam rose and fogged the blurry mirror, the mirror where you could never actually see your face anyway. They made them that way on purpose, for some reason...the mirror fogged, more and more. And then there was something moving in it, either in the fog or the mirror itself. The blurry silver sheen of it seemed to churn and roll.

"What the—"

Before Hayley could even finish her sentence, there were hands reaching for them out of the mirror, arms that were long and thin, hands made of water with reaching fingers that were longer and longer and terribly, terribly thin, thin as bones, thin as daggers—

And behind the hands was a long face in the mirror, grotesquely long with an open mouth and a chin dropping down so the mouth opened wider and wider—

Hayley was shrieking right in her ear at the top of her lungs. Cara turned and grabbed the door handle.

She wrenched it open, and both of them threw themselves through the crack, running at full tilt across the wet parking lot toward the road that led through the woods out to Route 6, pounding the wet pavement with their feet. Then they were running up the road, leaving the parking lot behind them. The rain was barely a mist now, Cara realized, and kept running, and then felt flooded with relief.

They were saved. There were Max's headlights.

Six

"OK. So that was not a Peeping Tom," said Hayley emphatically.

It was about two in the morning and they were home and warm. The three of them—Cara, Hayley, and Jax— sat in their dad's study by lamplight with blankets pulled around them, drinking hot chocolate with marshmallows in it. The library part of the study, behind the big desk with its jar full of Milk-Bones for Rufus, had two overstuffed arm-chairs, a fireplace with a marble mantelpiece and lion heads at both ends, and dusty old bookshelves on two of the walls. Cara had always thought it was a nice room. Beyond the chairs was a bay window that looked out over the water—or would if they didn't have the deep-red drapes pulled shut.

Max had insisted on driving back to the park and keeping vigil from the car with his friends, though Jax had made them promise not to go near the tent till dawn. Max had never seen the Pouring Man—the so-called *dead soldier*—which was why, Cara thought, he didn't take her story too seriously.

Though he hadn't said so, maybe he even thought she was imagining things.

"There's no way you're gonna convince me that thing coming out of the mirror was just some weirdo who likes spying on girls," went on Hayley.

"Not so much," admitted Jax.

He sat cross-legged on a thick rug on the floor and was eating sugary cereal from the box with his fingers. That was his habit when he was trying to think something through.

"I haven't been a hundred percent honest with you," said Cara to Hayley sheepishly.

"Yeah. No kidding."

"I'm sorry," Cara told her, and meant it.

Before this whole thing, she'd always thought of herself as pretty truthful, aside from the rare white lie to save someone's feelings. She wanted to have integrity.

"So what the hell was it?" asked Hayley. "I mean there was that—face thing in the mirror—and the hands were stretching out longer than any hands could ever be, like they were groping for us...."

"You said he was in the tapwater?" said Jax, turning to Cara.

Cara kept her own hands cupped around her mug of cocoa, alternating between sipping and blowing on it. She'd toweled off, so she wasn't still soaking, but both she and Hayley were wearing bathrobes and thick socks—Hayley had brought puffy pink bedroom slippers in her overnight bag—and had their hair wrapped up in soft towels.

"That was how he got in," she said to Jax, nodding. "Through the pipes. Not the door."

"Yeah, um, pipes? I'm not getting it," said Hayley.

"He travels through water," explained Cara. "He has to have water to travel. And he likes the nighttime, too. Maybe

132

there was enough wetness in the pipes that he could move through them? But then he turned to steam when he came out, because it was too bright or dry in the bathroom for him to, you know, *materialize* all the way...."

"Before that," said Jax, "you said he took the shape of Hayley?"

"He *did*," said Cara. "He really did! Jax, I swear. I was inside the tent, and she'd gone out across the parking lot to the bathroom, and I thought it was her. I heard these hands scratching and scrabbling, you know, trying to undo the zipper on the flap in the dark? And I turned my flashlight on them and they were *her* hands. Her fingers! They looked just like them! So I told her to come in."

"You invited him," said Jax.

"It was meant for Hayley. But I guess I did."

"I didn't know he could do that," said Jax. "Shapeshifting. He's more powerful than I thought, that's for sure."

"Wait," said Hayley. "*Shapeshifting?* But that's, like, the sci-fi channel! You guys have got to be kidding me."

"It's a kind of mind-control, I would guess," said Jax. "I can't be certain, of course, but that would be a more efficient strategy, to make the observer *think* he looks a certain way. He's not actually transmuting atoms or anything. 'Course, mind control's a pretty good trick too."

"Whatever!" said Hayley. "You guys need to tell me what's going on. I mean, he was after me, too, right?"

"He won't bother you unless you're with us," said Jax. "I'm pretty certain of that."

133

"And, of course, I mean, you can go home now, if you want to," said Cara. "I wouldn't blame you, that's for sure."

"I don't want to go home," said Hayley. "At least—not while it's still dark out. No thanks."

"You're pretty safe in here," said Jax.

"We think," added Cara.

"But then—what does he want from you?"

Jax turned to Cara, expectant.

"You know more now, don't you?" he said.

His eyes seemed to be taking her measure.

"I had a dream," she confessed. "A really realistic one. Mom was in it."

"Oh, *man*. The creepy guy has something to do with your mother?" asked Hayley.

"He's trying to keep us from her," said Cara.

She leaned forward and set her empty mug down on a table, on a stack of her dad's books. Then she sat back, feeling spacey…she twisted her favorite ring back and forth on her middle finger. Her mother had given it to her for her twelfth birthday: silver, with a round white and blue design that looked like an eye. She had said it was for good luck. *To ward off the evil eye*, her mother said.

"Um," said Hayley. "Like, why?"

Jax shook his head, then looked sideways, checking with Cara.

"We don't exactly know," he said.

"There's something going on," Cara told Hayley.

"Yeah, I got that much," said Hayley.

She was winding a strand of her yellow hair around a pencil.

"In the world. Beyond us. Some kind of a fight. And he's on one side and our mother is on the other. And we're supposed to be there, too. At least, I think that's what she was telling me.... We're supposed to be joining in the fight, but to do that we have to get to her. Or to the others, her friends, maybe? And she's trying to help us, but he doesn't want us to succeed, because he's one of the bad guys. She called him dead. *One of the dead soldiers,* is what she called him, though I don't know what she meant. She also said his name is fear. She said he works for the someone called the Cold Man. Or wait, the Cold *One...*"

Jax was gazing up at her from the floor, his cereal box forgotten, while Hayley stared from her armchair, Cara's mother's terrycloth bathrobe swamping her small frame.

"Huh. Well, you said a mouthful," said Hayley.

There was a pause. Cara was overwhelmed herself—where had all that come from? She hadn't thought about the whole thing before at all, at least not consciously.

"That's more than I knew," said Jax after a moment.

"She also said...," started Cara, and turned to Jax. She hesitated, and then decided to take the plunge. "She said the visionary is me," she went on.

She felt a little proud of it—the pride kind of escaped her control, surged up despite herself—but there was no good reason for that except being conceited, she reminded herself. It was only a dream, after all. *Her* dream.

135

Basically, *she* was the one who suddenly had the idea that she was the visionary. It wasn't like her mother had come up and said it to all of them, in the flesh.

Usually, in their family, it was Jax who knew things. It was Max who did things—sports, popularity, whatever—and it was Jax who knew things. She only half-believed she'd been singled out at all, frankly.

But then Jax surprised her.

"I suspected as much," he said. "You see things. I hear them and I think about them. I'm more of an interpreter type."

"You guys lost me again," said Hayley, shaking her head in resignation.

"So Max is the arbiter? I wouldn't want Max judging *me*," said Cara. "Geez."

"No kidding," said Jax.

"Max is some kind of a judge?" asked Hayley. "In your game here?"

"It's not a game," said Jax. "Did the guy in the mirror seem like a game to you?"

"I wish it was a game," said Cara.

"Max would make a good judge, actually," said Hayley, and picked a mint-green marshmallow out of her cocoa, scrutinizing it.

"She has a major crush on him," Cara told Jax, her eyes rolling.

"No, but for real," said Hayley. "You're kind of harsh on him. This summer, anyway. But he's just trying to stay cool.

It makes him lonely, but he has to, to keep it together. And he's really a fair person, you know that? He's always jumping in to make sure big guys don't pick on little ones. You guys are way harsh."

She shook her head and popped the marshmallow into her mouth.

Jax and Cara exchanged glances. Hayley might have a point, Cara thought with a pang of guilt—although Max could make himself pretty hard to be nice to when he was always locked up in his room wearing headphones. Or at the park jumping his skateboard. Again and again and again…

Still. He had his own way of dealing, and the past months hadn't been easy for him either. Hayley was right about that part.

"Be that as it may," said Jax.

"She said she couldn't make it simpler for us," said Cara. "Because just like you thought, Jax, he can read us, or at least read you, so as soon as *we* know where she is, *he'll* know, too. So it's got to be, like, this last-minute thing, somehow. The way we find her, I mean. It can't be a slow hunt. She has to be revealed to us when we're not expecting it, basically. Or something like that."

"That does make it hard," said Jax.

"I don't know about you guys," said Hayley, yawning, "but I kind of need to crash."

"Keep the phone nearby, Jax," said Cara, rising from her armchair. "And wake us up if it rings."

Jax nodded quickly, anxious to be responsible despite being the one who'd been left at home like a baby.

"Will do," he said.

⚏

They slept in so late that it was almost noon by the time Cara sat up in her double bed to blink at the fringe of bright sunlight around the window blinds.

She'd been woken by the jangling sound of Max and his friends banging in through the front door; now she could hear them downstairs. She sat listening as they went through the kitchen, opening and slamming cabinets and drawers. No doubt they were prowling through every available storage space looking for junk food.

She heard them laughing at the bottom of the stairs and had to assume that their night, at least, had been relaxed and uneventful.

"What time is it?" asked Hayley sleepily, opening one eye and stretching beneath the coverlet.

"Late," said Cara. "And Max is home, so I guess that means you're going to get right up and put your makeup on."

"Shut *up*," said Hayley, but she got out of bed, tossed on her pink robe, and padded into the bathroom in her cat-paw slippers. Cara heard the tap running and the sound of an electric toothbrush. Slippers, robe, electric toothbrush—Hayley didn't travel light.

"Is everyone decent?" said Jax from the door.

Hayley closed herself in the bathroom, a bit of a prude considering the intruder was only ten. Then again, Hayley didn't have brothers. She wasn't used to the lack of privacy.

"It's fine," called Cara. "It's just me."

Jax opened the door and entered, fully dressed in what looked like yesterday's clothes, with Rufus beside him.

"So they didn't see anything during the night, right?" asked Cara.

Jax shook his head as the dog licked Cara's outstretched hand, then bounded over to his favorite spot on the rug and curled up. Cara got out of bed and opened the blinds, flooding her bedroom with light.

The day, for once, was blue and clear. The water of the bay sparkled, stretched out beneath her.

She opened the window and cool, clean air swept in. She breathed deeply. Now that it wasn't raining, she could leave it open....

"Listen, Car," said Jax in a low voice, glancing quickly at the bathroom door. "The thing is, he's getter stronger. Because it's almost a new moon. You know, when the sky is darkest? In a sense, when it's the deepest night."

"What, like vampires or werewolves or something? He's hooked up to the phases of the moon?"

"Yeah, like all the soldiers," he nodded. "Like all the soldiers in the army of the dark," he added ominously.

"You made that up," said Cara.

"Nah, actually it's a line from a game. I thought it sounded good. But the deal with him is, he hates the full moon, because it sheds light. It sort of turns night into day."

"So then when's this new moon coming?" asked Cara, going over to her closet, opening it, and staring in at the rack of empty hangers. Clean clothes were often hard to find since her mother had left.

"Problem is, it's tonight."

"What can we do?"

"Just be careful, I guess," said Jax, but his small face was tight with concern.

"Like for instance don't say 'Come in' to the bad guy, you mean?"

Jax sat down by Rufus, rubbing between the floppy ears.

"I'm not even happy about you and Max being out at night, with him there. But I guess you have to be. Right?"

"Well, there's no other way to see the ocean," said Cara.

"Actually," said Jax thoughtfully, "there just might be. You can pull down satellite images—there's a famous one of a red tide in California, so I know those phytoplankton can show up in the dark. In the picture I'm thinking of, you can see this bright turquoise color and the red, too, from way up in the stratosphere. Or thermosphere, technically. Or exosphere..."

"Talk normally."

"In low-earth orbit the satellites are still above the stratosphere, 200 kilometers up at a minimum...or else you get this rapid orbital decay—"

"Jax. Stop already."

"Anyway, I'll check it out."

"You're telling me we can look at Marconi from, like, outer space?"

"Maybe not us, not in real time," said Jax. "We don't exactly have top-level access. Google, for example, uses old satellite photos. But I might be able to get in using Mom's account. Let me check, anyway."

"I'm not going out there tonight unless I have to," said Cara and turned from Jax to pull on a tank top. "Max should go again. Nothing ever happens to him. He's lucky."

"I'm amazed Max is even going along with all this," said Jax. "For that reason if nothing else: things don't seem to happen to him. It's like he's outside it...."

"He saw you with the leatherback," said Cara. "That's the only thing he's ever witnessed that makes him think we're not just playing."

"And then the pirate ship," said Jax. "He's probably doing it just because of that, at this point."

"Would you two stop ragging on him?" said Hayley, stepping out of the bathroom fully dressed and with her trademark shiny lip gloss and eyeliner already applied.

"We're not ragging at all," objected Cara.

"You are, too," argued Hayley, flipping her hair. "You act like it's you two against him."

Cara and Jax looked at each other—Cara, at least, registering that maybe what she said was true.

"He's a skeptic," said Jax.

"And we know that what we've seen is real," said Cara. "That's all."

"Huh," said Hayley. "Well, I'm going down to hang with the guys."

"Go for it," said Cara. "Just give me a minute."

Hayley went out, taking the staircase two steps at a time.

"She is *way* too young for him," said Jax severely.

—※—

Jax was still trying to get satellite feed from Marconi Beach up on his laptop in the late afternoon when Max left to get Zee's father's scuba stuff ready. He had all the gear—masks and fins, tanks and wet suits—so Max just had to get it prepped and ready for them to use.

And Hayley had long since gone home. As far as Cara could tell, she was more focused on Max and whether or not he might like her than the fact that they'd looked at a mirror and seen something supernatural that Jax said "practically defied the laws of physics and turned all of reality on its head."

Cara went into Jax's room and looked over his shoulder as he pulled up aerial photos of the Cape. Brown and green splotches that were treetops flashed across his screen, the black of rooftops and blue and brighter green of the water.

"You know what?" he exclaimed suddenly. "I got it! We should use the webcam! There's a webcam at Marconi. Surfers use it to check on the waves. The problem is, it hasn't been good surf conditions lately, so right now it's pointing in the wrong direction."

Onto his screen flashed a scene of the beach—not a satellite photo, from above, but a regular beach webcam. It was a view of the cliffs that rose over Marconi, to be exact. She saw the long flight of wooden stairs that went up from the water to the parking lot that overlooked it, on the clifftop.

"But it's pointing inland," said Cara.

"Right."

"But how can we—do we even know where it is? The actual camera?"

"I do. It's on the lifeguard station," said Jax. "I've seen it there. Halfway down the beach between the cliffs and the waterline, on that high platform where they sit. All we need to do is turn it around so it faces out to sea. Chances are no one would even notice till morning. Surfers don't care how the waves are doing in the middle of the night." He glanced fleetingly at the time readout on the upper corner of his display. "Shoot. It's getting late. I don't know if there's still time before dark."

Cara thought for a second. Max had taken the car, so he couldn't drive them. The bike ride took at least twenty minutes. She looked at her watch.

"We'd get there before sunset, definitely," she said.

"But on the way back...," said Jax, and trailed off.

"We have to risk it," she said. "Better than spending all night out there."

"Even if it was Max?"

If she and Jax went out now, and took the chance of riding home in the dark, Max wouldn't have to be out later, vulnerable.

"We need to do it," she said firmly. "You and me. Listen, Jax. Just because nothing has happened to him yet doesn't mean it couldn't."

Jax nodded, but she could tell he was nervous.

"Come on," she said. "We can do this."

They practically jumped their bikes off the front porch, pedaling swiftly up the road toward Route 6; but as they got closer and closer it became clear that they had a rare, off-season traffic jam to contend with.

Cars were lined up along the highway at a complete standstill. The fumes from their idling engines filled the air, and a few horns honked way down the line.

"Oh, no," groaned Jax.

The cars wouldn't stop them, since they were on their bicycles, but the traffic jam would make the trip a lot less pleasant.

Suddenly she heard the whine of a siren behind them, and then an ambulance careened by at high speed.

"An accident," said Cara, feeling a chill.

And just like that, she knew there was something wrong. She had to find out what.

"Follow me," she said to Jax over her shoulder, and took off on her bike in the direction the ambulance had gone, toward the Wellfleet town center. She wove between the stopped cars to get across, then raced up the shoulder.

"Wait up!" Jax was calling behind her.

It was the opposite direction from Marconi.

She yelled back to him to explain, but what she said was probably lost to their velocity. He followed anyway, pedaling behind her as fast as his short, thin legs could go, a puzzled look on his face.

And then she saw it: beside the road, up ahead, a car was wrapped around a tree. A car that looked familiar.

Because it was theirs.

⚏

Cara had never felt so afraid, not even when the Pouring Man reached out. Never. The fear lodged in the pit of her stomach, making her almost sick.

When they got to the scene, there was the family car, the front of it forked so far into a tree trunk it looked as though the tree was part of it now. Then there was a police car, lights flashing, parked near the tree, and the ambulance pulled up with the back doors open. Then they saw the stretcher. And the prone form of a boy lying on it.

Max.

She practically threw herself off her bike, let it fall to the gravel and left the wheels spinning as she ran to the stretcher, which they were about to lift into the open back of the ambulance. She had eyes for no one but her brother...she couldn't see any blood, at least—a good sign, she told herself—and then she was looking down at him, ignoring the paramedics or whoever they were, who were saying things in her ear she didn't listen to.

"It's me, it's me," she heard her voice repeat, and she was bending over to look into the familiar face.

It was white, but his eyes were open.

"Cara?"

"Oh my *God*," she said, and her voice caught in her throat. Tears filled her eyes but didn't spill out. Her legs felt shaky with relief, or shock, or something. He was OK.

She almost had to sit down, she was shaking so hard.

"Your brother's one hell of a lucky kid," a paramedic was telling her, and put an around her trembly shoulders. It was a lady paramedic, bulky and kind-sounding. "He's got a broken arm, maybe a very mild concussion. And that's all."

"Never seen anything like it," someone was saying behind her to someone else. "It shoulda been way worse. Miracle the kid's still kicking."

"Max. What *happened*?"

Max tried to smile, which looked kind of pathetic but made the tears slide down her cheeks for some reason.

"Guess Dad won't leave me in charge again," he managed weakly.

"Don't joke! You never have accidents!"

His smile faded, and his eyes seemed to lose focus. The paramedic lady squeezed Cara's arm.

"Honey, it's just a broken arm," she said. "Really. You don't need to worry about him."

"…finally met your friend," Max was whispering.

"They'll keep him overnight after they set the arm, no doubt," said the paramedic. "You kids got a ride over there?"

Cara heard Jax answer her but couldn't listen to either of them. She leaned close over Max, whose lips were moving but whose faint words she couldn't hear in all the hubbub around her.

"What did you say?" she hissed, her lips a couple of inches from his ear.

"I think I met your friend," he whispered back. "What did you call him? The man who walks in water...."

Cara felt strange; all over her body her skin was tingling.

"He was here? He did this?"

"He came up out of nowhere," whispered Max, and then winced. Maybe they hadn't given him anything for the arm, because he seemed to be in pain.

"He came up?"

"First he was in the rearview mirror," murmured Max. "*Smiling*. Smiling this...awful smile."

"He was in the car with you?"

"No. He was just in the mirror—when I turned around there was no one in the back. And then..."

"Then?"

"Then when I turned to the front again, he was crouched on the hood. His face was a few inches away."

"Oh, no," said Cara.

"I swerved. I hit a tree."

"Of course you did. That was what he wanted," put in Jax, at her elbow.

The paramedics made them move out of the way as they heaved the stretcher up. Cara watched as Max grimaced.

"He did it so you wouldn't be with us tonight," said Jax loudly. "He was taking you out."

"*Who* was taking him out?" asked a policeman sharply, standing a bit behind them.

Cara shot Jax a look.

"We're just goofing, Officer," said Jax.

For some reason the policeman reached out and tousled Jax's hair, like he was cute. It was weird: Jax was acting like Max's accident didn't scare him at all, like it was nothing.

The ambulance pulled away with Max inside. Cara watched it go and then turned to Jax. The policeman had walked away, talking on his cell phone.

"*Goofing?*" hissed Cara under her breath.

Sometimes, while trying to pass for normal, Jax impersonated an idiot.

"We're riding with those guys," he explained to her. "The policemen? They'll take us to the hospital to be with Max. And I got an idea to make them stop at Marconi on the way so I can reposition the webcam."

"Poor Max," said Cara, biting her lip. "Did you see the look on his face? And he could have been—I mean, it could have been way worse, Jax. I can't believe you're not more freaked out."

"I know it could," he said, and looked determined. "But it wasn't. And we have to keep going."

"I don't get how the—how he did it," said Cara. "It wasn't raining! And it wasn't night yet, either!"

"I told you, he's more powerful today," said Jax. "He must have moved through another kind of water, somehow."

He walked to the side of the road and looked down.

"There's a creek right here, going under the road," he said. "See? There."

Cara stood beside him at the guardrail, looking down at a muddy trickle of water running into a culvert beneath them.

"He must have come in that," said Jax. "Maybe he could even materialize just for an instant outside the water, because he's getting stronger...."

"Hey, kid," said the policeman with the cell. "We'll cruise along behind you, why don't you drop those bikes back at home. Leave 'em here, they won't last till you get back."

"Thanks, Officer," said Jax, and they bent to grab the bars of their cycles.

※

The hospital was a lot of waiting around in white rooms that smelled a particular way—not bad but not really good, either. Zee showed up, too, with her fisherman dad, who'd driven her there. He *was* the man from the cheeseburger place—the bearded, sunburnt guy who knew about the algae in the red tides. He was nice enough, though he didn't recognize Cara.

At a vending machine off the lounge, when she and Zee were buying a soda, Zee leaned in close to her and whispered.

"So, what are you going to do if it's tonight?"

"I don't know! Can you get the scuba stuff for us? And maybe leave it somewhere?"

"It's really expensive," said Zee. "What if something happened to it? I'd be grounded till I was, like, wearing Depends."

"I know," said Cara. "I understand, I really do. But this is so important."

"What," said Zee. "Jax's science project?"

"It's *more* than that," said Cara, her voice growing louder. She checked herself and was thinking what else to say when Zee's dad loomed suddenly behind them and asked Zee to get him a Mountain Dew. A few seconds later, Zee went into Max's room for her visit, and after that her dad hurried her out, saying something about traps, and they left.

Cara and Jax finally said good-bye to Max at around ten at night. His arm in a cast, he was falling asleep with a baseball game blaring on the TV. He'd be there till the next morning at least, a nurse told them, for observation because of the concussion, but she reassured them that the arm would be fine and Max mostly needed a good night's rest.

Cara felt bad for her dad, who was agonizing over his choice to leave them by themselves. They'd had to call him to tell him about the accident, and he was already on his way to the airport to get on a flight coming back. It was obvious that besides being really worried for Max, he thought the accident was his own fault.

She wanted to tell him about the Pouring Man—about all the strange events, so he would know this hadn't just been an example of reckless teen driving or something. But her dad was into being a *man of reason*, as Jax put it. He would think she needed intensive talk therapy, and possibly Zoloft.

Lolly picked them up at the hospital and drove them home, her grandson in a baby seat in the back of her car with Jax beside him.

"I am definitely staying with you tonight," she said. "I brought Manny's crib in the trunk. No buts about it."

"We figured," said Jax.

"Thanks, Lolly," said Cara.

She was leaning against the car window, gazing out at the passing lights along the highway and feeling very tired. She wondered how on earth, if they actually saw the blue-green light on the ocean and Max wasn't back at home yet, they would ever get out to the sunken ship by themselves.

Seven

They decided to take shifts in front of Jax's laptop, and because she had the first shift she also had the difficult task of waking her little brother at midnight.

Lolly was asleep upstairs with the baby, in their parents' room, and Cara had drunk some of her dad's coffee to stay up, so now she was wired and couldn't get to sleep.

Jax, on the other hand, was crabby about being woken, and then all but nodded off at the console, so she made him drink coffee, too. She found some old instant in the cupboard and added plenty of milk.

"Putrid," he said, and stuck his tongue out, eyes squeezed shut in revulsion. "I can't believe anyone drinks this stuff on purpose."

"I think there's Coke in the fridge," she said. "I'll get you that instead."

Soon Jax was wide awake and had his screen set up with two windows, one showing the webcam view, the other displaying one of his databases.

"Why don't you try to sleep," he said. "You need it."

But it was no good. She sat up in her bed, the bedside light on, and kept getting up to do things—first to make herself a PB and J, then to pace the kitchen worrying about

Max and what other things the Pouring Man could do to them. If he could do that, was there a limit?

She still felt mad at her mother sometimes—at moments like this when she was stressed out. She was just a kid; they all were, even Max. It wasn't fair they had to save her. She should be saving *them*. Their mother should be here, and *she* should protect *them* from the so-called *man whose name was fear*, for God's sake.

Then she felt bad for thinking that way. They weren't really kids, after all—or barely, anymore, except for Jax who was a freak of nature in any case and had a mental age of 90—and their mother had always looked after everything, and now it was their turn.

But still, as she paced, she went back and forth between feeling sorry for herself and Max and Jax and her mother and feeling angry. She couldn't seem to help it.

"Max could have been *killed*," she said aloud, standing still in the middle of the kitchen. It was like she was accusing someone.

She was alone, of course.

⚏

She must have fallen asleep, because the next thing she knew Jax was standing over her, where she was curled in her dad's favorite armchair, and he had his laptop open.

"Do you see something?" he asked, and crouched down beside her to show her the display.

She rubbed her eyes and looked at the screen, which was basically a rectangle of black. In the middle of the black she saw a faint lightness, but she wasn't sure if it was anything—it might just be the reflection of a passing plane on the waves, or a faraway boat. It might be anything, in fact.

"I don't know," she said, doubtful.

"What if it *is*?" said Jax.

"I mean, it could be," said Cara. She tried to look more closely, but the light was so faint, so characterless, that she couldn't decide. "Or it could be nothing."

She didn't *want* it to be the fires, of course. She didn't want it to be what they were looking for. Because if it was, they'd have to tackle it without Max.

But then she thought, what if we miss it? Because we're afraid to handle it without him? What if we miss our *one chance*?

She sat up straighter in the chair, touching her good-luck ring with two fingers of the other hand. It grounded her, somehow. Her mother had called it a name in a foreign language, she recalled—nazam, or nazar, she thought now. Not that it mattered...but as she touched the ring, staring out in front of her over the top of the computer at her dad's bookcase, she found the spines of the history books faded from her sight, and she could imagine, instead, the scene on the ocean: a yellow, fluorescent buoy bobbing on the water and all around it what looked like a bright field—a shining field. Beneath the field, columns of blue-green light went down, down into the water, and the waves moved around her....

"What's wrong?" asked Jax.

She was dizzy and had lurched sideways in her chair.

"Seasick," she said, because it came into her head.

It must be true.

And she rose.

"You're right," she said. "We have to go. It's time."

⧈

Once, when their dad was on a health kick and didn't want to drive so much, he had put together a strange cart that attached to the back of his bicycle. It looked a bit like the buggies people pulled their babies around in, but it was meant to hold a kayak. He'd only used it for short distances, mostly to get to the bayside beaches near their house when he wanted to go for a paddle by himself. His kayaks were very light, and so long they could be hard to balance without scraping occasionally on the ground, but the cart had worked for their dad, and it would work, she hoped, for them too.

But she and Jax had to go farther—across the highway to the ocean side. She didn't remember her dad doing that.

They took one of the doubles, a wooden kayak their dad had built last summer from a kit when he was trying to relax more and not work so much. He called it a pygmy boat or something; since it was a double, it could easily hold both of them. They roped it onto the cart carefully, because if it fell off in the dark, on the beach road, it might be hard to get back on. They threw in paddles, water and lights and

156

Cara's backpack; they wore their headlamps from camping trips, just in case.

Cara would pull the kayak behind her, with Jax up ahead to scout out the smoothest route.

And finally she called Zee's cell, to find out how they could pick up the scuba and night-diving gear in case they turned out to need it. She had no idea what to do if Zee said no—she could call Cory, she guessed, but it would be beyond weird coming out of the blue like this....

It took a long time for Zee to pick up, and when she did she sounded half asleep. But the scuba stuff was laid out in her garage, she said in a smudged, groggy voice. The tanks were all full and had been checked. There were flashlights and headlamps you could use underwater. If Cara and Jax were quiet, they could come pick it up on their way; the garage door was unlocked.

"OK," said Jax, putting on his helmet on the porch. Her bike was on the road already, the kayak secured behind it. "Then let's rock and roll."

He was trying to sound like Max, man of action. With Max in the hospital and her dad in the air somewhere between here and Chicago, Jax must think he was supposed to act like the man of the house.

As they passed Hayley's place, cycling tentatively as Cara got used to towing the kayak behind her, a porch light blinked on. Surprised, they braked and watched as Hayley slipped out the front door and ran down the walkway to meet them.

"I heard about Max," she said. "He's OK, right?"

"His arm is broken," said Cara. "But that's it. He'll be home tomorrow, and you can draw a cutesy heart on his cast."

"Is it happening now? The thing with the sea lights?"

"We think it might be," said Jax.

"We're not sure," put in Cara. "We have to check it out, is all."

"But you can't go without Max," said Hayley urgently. "He's—you need him to stay safe! You can't go out there without him!"

"We have to," said Cara. "He's in the hospital. He's *unconscious*. And this could be it. This could be our chance."

"But—"

"We do have to," said Jax gravely.

No one said anything for a few seconds.

"Then *I'm* coming," said Hayley.

"That's crazy," said Cara. "It could be *dangerous*. Have you already forgotten?"

"You might need me. It was supposed to be three, remember? And now there's only two of you. So count me in."

Cara and Jax turned toward each other, but she couldn't see the expression on his face in the dark.

"OK, get your bike," he said after a moment, decisive. "I'll go back and get you a life vest, so you don't sink."

In five minutes they had three bikes and were on their way again. Cara didn't know what she thought about Hayley being with them, but the message had said three, that was true. Tonight might not be the time, in any case. She hoped it proved not to be—hoped it was a false alarm, so the real action could wait until Max was back.

It seemed like a long, dark ride to Zee's place, and once there they could barely fit the gear and the wetsuits into the kayak. Finally all of it was bundled in, though, and they lowered the garage door with a creak. Then they had to cross Route 6, and turns were the hardest part. But finally they were making their slow way up the lonely road that cut through the national seashore to the beach. It had no streetlamps, being a park road, and the moon was gone, covered in black. The lights on their bikes were solitary in the dimness around them—a dimness full of the sighing of the breeze through short pines, the rubber of their tires on the pavement, the rubbing of the kayak against its bungee cords....

Cara found herself counting, at times, in her head, to ward off thoughts of the Pouring Man. He could appear anytime, couldn't he, now that it was dark out? Wasn't that what they'd found out today? On the Cape, after all, water could pop up anytime.

But at long last, when Cara's phone said two in the morning, they made it to the parking lot and left their bikes lying on the sidewalk. Maybe having their bikes stolen was the least of their worries. They untied the kayak and carried the boat and its contents, with some awkwardness, down the steep wooden staircase to the sandy flat of the beach. It dropped once, but luckily it slid only a few steps before it stuck, and they were able to pick it up again.

As they sidestepped down the stairs, she looked out over the water. Far out in front of them was a glow—a pale and otherworldly green.

⸙

They pulled on the wet suits first, which were too big for them and felt heavy. Hayley had done some scuba once before—something called a "resort dive" a while back on a Bahamas vacation, when her dad was still around and the family had some money—so she offered to go in, if they needed her to, but Cara and Jax shook their heads. It was hard to figure out how to fit into the kayaks with tanks on their backs, especially since there were only two seats and Hayley had to be crammed into the same seat as Jax, but finally they figured it out and Cara pushed out the boat and then jumped in herself.

With Cara and Jax handling the paddles and Hayley trailing her arms not so helpfully in the water, they headed straight out toward the patch of light. Their wet, bare feet, awaiting the fins, were braced against the footrests and Cara felt how fragile they were, in a way—three kids in a pygmy boat, balanced there tenuously, out in the middle of nowhere, on the vast, dark kingdom of the ocean.

At first they heard nothing but the soft, low curling-under sound of the waves hitting the sand behind them. Then that sound faded out as they drew farther away from shore, and there was only the rhythmic scoop and splash of their paddles and the slosh of water against the kayak's hull. For once, Hayley didn't say much.

Cara's stomach felt hollow with nerves. She wished Max were here—Max with his scuba knowledge and his common sense, his casual, skeptical attitude that somehow inspired confidence. She almost wanted to call him at the hospital, just to be reassured by his voice; and technically she could if she wanted to, because there was a strong enough signal out here and Jax, of course, always had his cell in his pocket. Or in this case in a dry bag, at least.

But Max was asleep in a well-lit building on solid ground, his arm in a sling and an IV stuck into him with a button he could push if he decided he needed pain relief, and he deserved to rest. Anyway, if she called him now he'd be furious that they were going without him—furious both that he was being left out and that they were taking such a big risk.

If this turned out not to be a false alarm, she would simply have to do it without him—she would have to be the eldest, the responsible one.

And yet, at the same time, she had to trust herself to Jax—Jax and his wild instincts. Commit her belief utterly to a ten-year-old, in a matter that could be life or death.

Something compelled her forward. She had to do this; she couldn't give up. She was needed.

She closed her eyes as she lifted, dropped, and raised the paddle again, as she dipped it on the other side. It wasn't much harder than paddling with her eyes wide open, at the moment: there were no obstacles, and no moon over the wide-open dark water. For some reason she thought of "The Owl and the Pussycat," which she had loved when she was a little girl and her mother read it to her at bedtime: *The Owl and the Pussy-cat went to sea in a beautiful pea-green boat...They danced by the light of the moon, the moon, they danced by the light of the moon.*

They were nearing the glow on the waves now, and it began to look like something unearthly—not the reflection of lights from boats or shore on the waves, nor the shine of starlight, that much she was sure of.

"Can anyone see the buoy?" asked Jax, who was farthest forward.

"Not yet," said Cara.

"Here," said Hayley, and snapped on one of the flashlights. Ahead of them her beam jumped on the water, but revealed nothing. "Oh well."

On and on, and briefly Cara turned and gazed back at the shore behind them, which looked almost as dark as the water, as far as she could see. A ways to the north there was one point of light, which she thought was maybe a restaurant called the Beachcomber—it was the only business on the beach side that she knew, up at Cahoon Hollow. It was built right over the water, a tourist trap, as her dad called it, and was always crowded in the high season. As far as she knew, it was the closest thing that would be lit up at night north of here...and then she heard a gasp: Hayley. She turned back around in time to see, gleaming ahead of them, an ocean that looked turquoise.

It was lit up like an aquarium. She couldn't tell whether the thrill she felt was one of excitement or plain fear.

She felt herself break out in a sweat—or maybe she just noticed that she was already sweating beneath the oversized wetsuit, which was awful to paddle in.

"That's it, Jax," she said.

"Has to be," he agreed.

"We're going to have to do it without Max."

They gazed at each other, not quite believing it.

"The buoy is yellow," she said after a minute. That was the way she had seen it. "Let's look for it."

"We need to tie the boat to the buoy," added Jax. "And Hayley, you'll be the lookout. Then, if we need you, we can pull on the anchor line and you can come in."

"Lookout? Alone?"

"Look," said Jax. "We don't know what we're doing. We may need someone out of the water, someone who could help if something happened to us. Because this—this is *his* domain."

There was a silence as Hayley waved her flashlight around; but it was swallowed up in the glow from the waves, no use at all.

"There," said Hayley, and pointed.

Sure enough, a yellow buoy floated a few feet away.

"I'll tie it," said Jax, and before they knew it he was doing an odd slither off the boat and into the water. The kayak rocked but didn't flip. Jax half groaned, half screeched. "Cold! It's so, so cold!"

"I can't believe you're doing this," said Hayley. "And I don't get it—how deep down is the wreck, anyway?"

"It's not supposed to be too deep," said Cara.

"Very shallow. About thirty feet," sputtered Jax from the water, working to attach the boat to the buoy. She could see his legs moving beneath the glowing water to keep him afloat, vague silhouettes. The kayak bobbed away from him for an instant, pulling the rope taut, and Cara steered them back with her paddle.

"There," he said, and then tied on another rope—a guide rope that was going down with them into the depths. He scrabbled with a hand in the front hatch of the kayak and brought out a donut-shaped weight, which he fixed to the end of the rope before he dropped it into the water.

"How'd you learn to tie all those knots?" asked Cara, surprised.

"We had a thing on knots at camp," said Jax, and then glugged some water by mistake and spat it out as he clung to the side. "They did a Boy Scout deal. So Hayley? We're going to need a signal, in case of emergency."

"How will you signal?"

"Three tugs in a row. And you can do it, too—tug on the rope if you need to," he told Hayley. "Three sharp tugs in a row if you want us to come up. If there's danger up here, danger to you, anything. I don't think you can pull us up—

it would capsize this thing. So if we signal, all it means is you should get out of here."

"And you can paddle back in to shore if we're not back in what—Jax?"

"It should be about two hours, since it's so shallow here. I mean, I think we have about two hours' worth of air. Cara, I'm going to need you to put my dive weights on me. After that I'll sink down. The belt's in the bottom there. So—let's do the masks first, OK? And then hand me my weights and I'll just drop..."

"Masks on," said Cara, and handed his over the side.

They adjusted the masks over their eyes and noses.

"Wait," said Cara, and propped hers up on her forehead. She felt suddenly panicky. "Jax. We don't have a clue what we're doing! We don't even know why we're going down there!"

"She needs us," said Jax, sounding pinched and nasal through the thick, cloudy plastic. "You know that, Car. That's why we're going."

Cara stared at him, but his eyes were invisible through the mask, in the dark. He stuck his regulator into his mouth and flicked on his headlamp.

Finally she took a deep breath, flicked on her own light, and put in her own mouthpiece.

"Good luck, guys," said Hayley. "Don't die on me."

Cara clicked her own weight belt on and handed Jax his, and as he grabbed them and sank, she reached up out and touched the back of Hayley's hand. Then she slid backward out of the kayak—as close to the backward roll Max had taught her as she could come without a normal diving boat.

Cold, cold, cold. Even with the wet suit on.

She got her bearings for a second, breathing the way Max had taught her, only through the mouth. *Now I'm a mouthbreather*, she thought. It wasn't so bad.

Jax was near her, a small, dark shape in the glowing green, moving downward. She saw his swim fins swishing.

She grabbed the rope and followed.

Eight

She concentrated on keeping a hand on the rope but pointing her head and shoulders downward. Curiously the water got warmer as she descended, or it felt that way to her, at least, which was the opposite of how she'd expected it to be.... There was so much color swirling around her that she couldn't see anything else at first—a lovely bright aqua color. She saw why the verse had called it fire, *the night of fires beneath the sea.*

The salt load made the seawater hard to see through, though: it was a mist of fine particles, glowing and swirling around her. Not like the clear water in a turquoise swimming pool; more like blooms and currents of light.

She and Jax had wikied the plankton, microscopic pictures that showed their shapes. They were beautiful, even the poisonous ones—lacy and delicate, shaped like acorns in some cases or diamonds or stars. Of course you could never see that unless you were looking at them under a microscope, she thought, but it was strange to think of those all around in the water, minuscule organisms, lifeforms entering her body and Jax's along with the water molecules—tiny beings like whole worlds, sculpted and fragile-looking though in fact they were powerful enough to give out this amazing glow....

And to make her and Jax pretty sick, possibly. If they were the toxic kind.

Hopefully they weren't.

She felt pressure on her head as she descended, but then it seemed to subside. Jax was ahead of her, farther down; she could just make out the wake that rose from his kicking fins. Down farther they swam, and she found she was thinking of her mother—would her mother somehow appear down here, gliding out of the dim fathoms like a mermaid? The dream had put the notion in her head—her mother swimming up through the turquoise water, reaching for them through the luminous particles.

Then she realized the thought was actually more alarming than comforting. She wanted the same mother back she'd always had—the real mother she'd always known, exactly the same as the day she vanished, not one iota different.

In the dream her mother's long hair had floated around her as though it was submerged...almost as though her mother, it occurred to her suddenly, had drowned.

No. Just because her mother had called her a visionary didn't mean that anything she thought of had to have some kind of deep meaning.

A dark mass loomed up: kelp, or seaweed that looked a lot like kelp, curling out of the depths. It had pods, rubbery pods on the end of stalks that were like long tentacles, waving beneath. The algae all around them lit up the underwater world, and she could see the bottom—sand littered with dark debris, with unfamiliar shapes.

Jax grabbed onto something at the bottom and looked up at her—a hard object, partially beneath the sand. He motioned for her to come over, too, and she grabbed it, her feet above her head, looking down and around, her free hand pushing the water. It was a piece of wood, maybe a rib of the boat.

They were floating in a half-illuminated country, dim in some places and then shining from the phosphorescence. The brightness receded into a murkier distance if she tried to fix her eyes on something far away, but the foreground was clear. Around them were the ship ruins—pieces of wood and metal, she thought, though she didn't know how the wood could be anything but rotten after three centuries underwater. A few small, dull-colored fish swam in and out and around.

There were rocks, too, piles of boulder-size rocks like small stone mountains on the sandy floor. From their cracks rose twisting columns of seaweed, stems emerging from the outcroppings where they were anchored and flowing overhead into a dark-green canopy. Their stems and leaves swayed gracefully with the slow currents near the bottom of the ocean. They were like forests.

The strangest thing about this kingdom of the sea, she thought, was how it was silent and loud at once.

Then, with the toes of his swim fins touching the sand, Jax unclipped the anchor weight from the guide rope and re-clipped the rope to his weight belt. There was enough slack for them to swim quite far without pulling the rope

taut, which they had to in case they needed to signal Hayley.

So here they were, she thought: thirty feet under the surface of the endless Atlantic, no adults knowing where she was, no safety net, and who knew what strange thing would come shooting out of the dark.... There had been great white sharks sighted, recently, in the waters off Chatham. Not only that, but—she'd heard it said—they were actually hunting people now. Their usual food was getting harder to find....

Chatham was fifteen miles away. Great whites, Jax told her once, could swim forty miles in an hour. When they were hungry.

She wished Max were here.

Jax was swimming among the fragments of the wreck. She moved more hesitantly than he did, touching the rope. She wished they'd brought a tool to communicate with— boards they could write on or something. She should have made an agreement with Jax, she realized, that he could ping her down here, that they could make an exception to his promise.

She was surprised she wasn't freezing. Maybe that was a bad sign—maybe when you didn't feel cold anymore that meant you had, what did they call it, frostbite? Or hypo- thermia?—and were about to go unconscious....

Of course. Jax was holding his waterproof watch up to her face, its digital readout lit up. He could actually type on the thing, which was blocky and huge over the arm of his

wet suit. For all she knew he could watch YouTube videos on it. She should have known he wouldn't come unprepared—even if he forgot to clue her in about it.

DONT B AFRD, read the watch's display.

She shook her head, giving him a thumbs-up. There was a surreal beauty here, with the glow all around—if you could overlook the danger lurking out there in the infinite dark water beyond this small patch of light.

The danger of *him*.

Jax went back to his watch, pressing a button on the side rapid-fire, and then lifted it up for her to see again.

I MEAN THEY WONT HURT US. UNLESS HE TELLS THEM TO.

She raised her hands to say: *What? Who?*

Jax typed again.

BHIND U.

Warily she turned herself around in the water with a dog-paddling motion and startled when she saw them—figures among the ruins. They looked like outlines of people, darker than the swirling light of the water but still see-through: outlines like pencil drawings with only the faintest washes of color filling them. They were dressed in ragged coats, some with hats, some with long things hanging at their sides—one at the front had a red coat, an old pistol with a silver handle stuck into his sash. A black hat with a peak at the front.

Many of them. A crowd. Maybe a hundred or more.

She turned back to Jax.

GHOSTS, read his watch. WHYDAHS CREW. THE 1 WITH HAT IS CAPTAIN. BLACK SAM BELLAMY.

She should be afraid—now it was *ghosts*?—but the thin, mangy figures weren't coming closer. They just hung there passively, moving in a way that was odd and almost imperceptible. They shifted in the water so that she saw not a progress forward or backward, not the regular motion of bodies, but a kind of series of snapshots, like stop-motion photography—a pattern or imprint, a series of microscopic differences in position.

She'd never believed in ghosts. Ghosts were just stories told to gullible kids around campfires, kids who wanted to be scared for a second while they were roasting marshmallows. But then...memories were a kind of ghost, she thought in passing—like her grandparents, whom she never knew but had pictures of in her head from old black-and-white photos.

So maybe, as memories were ghosts, so were ghosts also a form of memory.

Jax typed on his watch again and held it up.

THEY WERE THE PIRATES, she read. THAT WENT DOWN W/THE SHIP.

Pirates? Pirates and ghosts? It was a regular Halloween party.

The watch was too slow. It frustrated her. She moved her hand through the water and grabbed Jax's wrist, then tapped her own temple.

WANT ME 2 PING? he typed.

She nodded.

Then suddenly it was like listening to headphones—a voice playing right between her ears. She hadn't felt this before; before she hadn't been able to tell when Jax was reading her until he said something that betrayed it. But this, she understood, was different: not only reading but also speaking. It was like Jax had opened a two-way channel on a radio. And what came out didn't sound like his speaking voice at all. Which made sense, since there were no actual vocal cords involved. But it was bizarre. It took her a while to be able to make out the words properly. No one would have known it was a little boy talking to her; it was more like a clear singing.

They're bound here because they're in service to him. They don't want to be, but they are. The Pouring Man. The way the pirates lived, the wrong they did? It makes them his. It keeps them here. Like slaves.

How do you know all this? she asked.

But he was grabbing her arm.

The selkie has arrived.

She raised her head and looked—moving slowly and fluidly, it seemed, like everything underwater and like water itself. Among the waving stalks of the seaweed, above a rock covered in roots and old barnacles, a creature was hovering, gazing at them out of huge dark eyes in a pale, blue-gray face. Its upper body had the approximate shape of a woman—Cara thought of her idea of a mermaid—but her head was far larger than a woman's would be, in proportion to her body, and the face drew into a soft kind of snout toward the chin, like a seal's. The dark eyes were on either side instead of in front, as people's eyes were, and long black hair floated around. She looked solemn and wise, yet the big eyes also reminded Cara of a baby.

Jax motioned to Cara to stay close as they swam toward her. Her body, they saw, tapered into a tail like a seal's, like the lower half of a seal's body—not a fish tail but a gray one. She had long flippers for arms.

Jax thought to Cara as they swam: *I'll talk to her.*

They didn't have their third, though, the third person the verse had said had to be there. They didn't have their *arbiter*, someone impartial to decide.

And decide what, anyway?

She had no idea.

They were almost up to the selkie then, moving through the seaweed. It was darker in here, though the lighted particles still whirled. When the stalks brushed against Cara's arms as she passed they felt slick and rubbery. Under the twisted canopy were dark shadows cast by the silhouettes of the kelp forest against the glow of the algae; the shade and beams of radiance patterned everything she could see, made their surroundings as complicated and dense as a jungle. Cara had a hard time telling what things were.

The selkie reached out her flippers, which curled around them and drew them in—rough and soft at the same time, almost unbearably strange. It was a kind of formal embrace, it seemed to Cara. She thought how alien it felt to be so close to the creature—she'd never really touched an animal that wasn't a pet, save for a few crabs from tidal pools and Jax's pitiable frogs....

And the selkie wasn't quite animal anyway, of course. She was something else.

Cara realized she was tense, not because she thought the selkie would hurt them but because she'd never been close to anything so *other*. Next to the selkie, even the ghosts of long-dead pirates seemed almost normal. The selkie was not of this world, she knew—it was from myth; it was like meeting a dragon.

If myth were true, she thought—if all of it were true!

Jax's forehead was against the selkie's as though they were head-butting. Then he pulled away, bowing solemnly. And before Cara knew it the selkie was gone again, swooshed off into the darkness underneath the waving kelp.

Jax was pinging her.

She wants to give me the key, but she can't.

Why not? thought Cara.

Because he's coming now.

The water around them seemed suddenly colder.

Of *course* he was coming.

So? she thought at Jax, insistently. *Can't she just give it to us and then we can go? Get out of here and away from him?*

We have to make ourselves safe first. We have to stand up to him. If we can, he won't be able to get into our heads anymore. He won't have access to our minds. Then she can tell us what we need to know.

175

Stand up to him? How?

I'm not sure. But maybe the ghosts can help us.

The ghosts? The ghosts of pirates? We have to get help from them?

Behind him, in the gloom, the flickering forms of the ghosts shifted and weaved, faintly menacing but suspended.

She felt a tug of despair. Jax looked so small in front of her, so slight and babyish, his blond hair waving in the water, his small body, in the overlarge wet suit, dwarfed by the tank gear and the weight belt.

Here they were in this alien greenness, this universe unknown to them. No Max, no Dad, no anyone—

No one else even knew where they were. No one knew they were here in the deep, here in the ocean where even grown people drowned.

She'd never felt so alone.

The cold and the Pouring Man, making his way toward them. When they were down here, surrounded by water—breathing his element. At their very weakest.

And all these ghosts at his command. These ghosts who had been cruel while they lived, and probably could be cruel now.

It was frustrating. It seemed practically impossible, to push out fear.

And if she and Jax lost, if they lost....

But Jax? What happens if we lose?

Don't think about that, he told her steadily. *He's coming now. And we can't run. We can't move. We have to stand up to him, whether the ghosts fight for him or for us. Just don't give in to fear.*

I need to know, Jax. Now it's your turn to tell me every-thing. What happens if we lose?

There was a silence between them, a blankness. And then:

It's simple: if we lose, then we're his, thought Jax heavily. *We're pressed into service. We join him.*

She shivered despite herself. Slowly she raised her hands in front of her, her fingers whiter than paper, wrinkled as an old, old lady's. Behind the white hands, the dark ghosts in their slow and shifting field.

⊰⊱

They anchored themselves next to the rope, directly under the buoy again. She didn't know why, except that it seemed, in a way, closest to home—closest to the only thing that was familiar: the kayak their dad had built.

And she grabbed one of Jax's hands. If she could keep hold of his hand, she was thinking, that would help, anyway. His fingers were pruney like her own. She held them tightly.

And when he raised the other hand and pointed, her heart leaped into her throat.

Across the sand, from out of the gloom where the brightness barely reached, the Pouring Man was walking toward them. Just walking, impossibly, on the bottom of the ocean. His clothing floated around him, but it seemed to be rags, black rags, and nothing else about him floated at

177

all. Not even his hair. It was still plastered down over his forehead, as though it was soaked in a way that not even the ocean tides could touch.

His feet hit on the sandy bottom, placed one in front of the other, deliberately and surely, and the sand rose around him in soundless dusty clouds.

He smiled, she saw, but it was not a smile you wanted to see. Not at all.

As he got closer and closer, walking ploddingly with a slow-motion gait, the smile exposed his teeth. His upper lip was pulled back in a snarl.

Still he came, and she knew she was squeezing Jax's hand so hard she might be hurting it, but she couldn't help herself.

He walked right through the ghosts, when he was close enough—walked through them like they were nothing at all, and they scattered at his approach, shifted away from him, slinking and cowering as though, at any moment, he might hit them.

His teeth were sharp, she saw when he was only a few feet away. She was mostly looking down across the sand, trying to contain her dread by looking at the ground instead of up at him. She couldn't close her eyes, she knew—that would not be facing him, as she must—but she didn't have to stare right at him, did she?

She did. She did, for all of them.

She forced herself to look up again. The colorless eyes. The teeth that came to points. The blue, rubbery lips.

I know you, she thought. *You're the dead soldier. Your name is fear. My mother told me about you.*

And he nodded. Unhurried, the way all things seemed to happen here. He moved his head up and then down with a kind of condescension, as though she was a stupid child and he was humoring her.

Your name is fear, she thought. *I am afraid of you.*

No! thought Jax. *No!*

But she shook her head. *You can't beat fear if you don't admit to it. So I admit it. But I won't run. You won't get me.*

His smile seemed to waver a bit, but then strengthened again. He was near them, maybe six feet away, maybe five...four...three....

Behind him the ghosts pulled in and rose up, a crowd at his back. They were so close now she could see some of their faces—pitted with scars, mouths of stained and missing teeth, some wearing eye patches like kids in Halloween costumes.

You won't get my brother. You won't get either of us, she thought, fighting against the strong desire to close her eyes, no matter how useless it would be.

He was right there. He was so close that he filled her vision. His cold face, the angry eyes.

We are afraid, she thought forcefully, *but here we are anyway. See? We won't run from you.*

And then he was on them. And filtering inside. Leaking in. Through the holes and the skin.

She felt his sour essence move through her mouth and down her throat, through the holes of her nose and ears, through her pores, the follicles of her hair, her fingernails. She felt a sickness in her scalp and lungs and at the pit of her stomach, right through the rubber of the wetsuit, from her hips down her legs all the way to her feet, from her shoulders to her fingertips. She felt it in the very ends of her bones—her skeleton, she guessed, as though he *lived* in it.

He filled her with his rotting sickness, his creeping paralysis. She couldn't move.

That was what he did, she understood in a rush—he made it so you couldn't move, you couldn't do anything. You were mostly water, after all, and so he could move through *you*—not just the world, but your body. She remembered it from biology: *the human body is up to 78 percent water*…and then you had no independence. She didn't even know if she was holding on to Jax's hand anymore; nor did she feel the reassuring grain of the sand on the fins. All that was gone, all contact with the outside. It was as though she had no center.

She was pure chaos. The chaos of terror.

And then there were terrible scenes—scenes she called up, scenes she saw, but scenes she also knew were true, that had happened, scenes from actual history. She saw the pirates on their ship, their ship that had once held a cargo of helpless slaves; she saw the vicious fights at sea, the blood and dirt and the violence that was casual for them. She saw them kill, with guns, knives, bare hands; she saw them hurt when they didn't even need to—people who couldn't fight back, people without weapons. She saw it when she didn't want to, and because it was inside her she couldn't shut it out by closing her eyes....

She was shaking, she knew, but the sensation was far away, someplace she couldn't quite be right now. She thought to herself: *It's not that it isn't real. But it doesn't have to be. It doesn't have to be the world.*

And she forced herself to look hard—so hard she thought her eyes were burning. Was it evil? Was it that people were evil, to do these things to each other?

They called them pirates like it was glamorous or something, almost a joke, really, but they were just gangsters who hurt and killed people. The gangsters of their time. How could she get through to them?

Forgive, she thought. The pirates had done all the worst things, and those worst things bound them to the Pouring Man. But if she could forgive them, maybe they'd listen.

But how to forgive them? *How?*

And then she saw the pirates when they were kids. She saw, in one long rush like a deep fast-forward, a movie that sped through her in swift flashes of perception, the ugly history of their lives. She saw how they were born and how they were hurt, the dingy spaces they barely lived in, the cruel figures that inhabited those small and stinking rooms. She saw how meanness made them feel alone, how the whole world turned into their enemy slowly because they made the wrong choices. And finally that left them here, the unloved and unloving, the criminals that hovered here as ghosts.

They'd lost themselves, she thought. They'd lost their own souls, if that was what you called it—those pieces of themselves that felt pity for other people. The pieces that could love, the pieces that were kind.

They weren't strong enough, and they were weak when they were hurt, and they couldn't say no to any of it.

That's what it is, she realized. You have to be strong enough to say no.

The viciousness came from being weak.

The scene flashed away for a second, and instead of it there was the face of the Pouring Man. Frowning.

Was that the pressure of Jax's hand? Maybe. It made her feel better.

You are losing, she told the Pouring Man, and as she thought it she felt an enormous grief flow through her for all the people who never had a chance to be happy, to be who they wanted to be, to live in the world without being made of pain. The grief was almost an ache, so powerful, so glittering and moving like a clean, fast river, that it made her forget to be scared.

I can see past what you want me to see, she thought. *I can see what people want to be.*

The river kept flowing through her, and then the Pouring Man was a few feet away. He had receded a bit. His frown was angry now, his teeth bared as though he was going to leap forward and tear open her throat.

No, she said, and felt sensation slowly creep back into

her arms and legs like the tingle after your foot fell asleep. That *was* Jax, holding her hand—she was sure of it.

A kid would turn away, she thought. A kid who was too weak to stand up to the bad guys. And some people stayed kids forever, even though they grew old. They grew old but they never grew up. They never got stronger at all.

I *want* to turn away, she thought. Who wouldn't?

But I won't.

This isn't your world, she told the Pouring Man. She felt as though she was speaking clearly through the thickness of the salt, through the liquid, the words flowing out of her mind with the force of objects. *It isn't his world*, she thought to the ghosts, who streamed from him now, streamed from his shoulders and his hands and arms like dark flags into the water, shapeless, flapping things. *It doesn't have to be.*

And then she was back. Her body was hers again; he had withdrawn his sourness from her flesh and blood in a shocking split-second, leaving her warm and full of energy. She was here in the water, only a couple of miles from her home, holding Jax's hand.

And the ghosts were on the Pouring Man. They were clawing and shredding at him, his arms, his shoulders, his face and his head. They had their hook hands into his black rags, their knives and swords shoved into him, all over him from every possible angle. They mobbed him.

The ghosts were on her side.

We've won their loyalty, thought Jax to her. *You did it.*

They can't kill him, though, because he's not alive. All they can do is stop him for a while.

In no time the Pouring Man seemed to be falling apart. He was peeling, splitting down the middle.

As they watched he was *rended*—that was the word that came to her. He was ripped into parts as though his body was soft—stringy in the middle, stringy as the sides of him split off and dark fragments floated in disarray. There was no blood, nothing like that, because, she guessed, he didn't have any; and as he split and drifted, the ghosts shrank back into the shadows.

She turned and looked at Jax, and she thought he was smiling, or would have been if the regulator wasn't blocking his mouth. But then his expression changed, and she looked where he was looking.

Because the dark fragments that had been the Pouring Man were drifting together again, piece by piece. They made two columns in the water, two small columns; they were turning into something. Not into him, but into two people. They gathered and became more solid and more colorful. They shaped into figures of children—children wearing scuba gear. Children with masks on, and oxygen tanks on their backs. One with long hair, the other shorter and blond.

Her and Jax, in fact.

She was looking at two kids who might as well be their own reflections. Like a mirror image.

Except for their eerie smiles. The other children didn't have to close their mouths around the regulators to breathe.

They simply smiled, with water flowing through them. And Cara recognized those smiles, because they weren't the smiles of kids.

The smiles were his.

She looked at Jax, trembling. He pointed upward, and in that same moment the copies began to rise. They didn't swim, didn't even move their arms: their arms, like the Pouring Man's before them, hung at their sides, motionless. Despite this they rose through the water.

Jax let go of her hand and fumbled to unclip his weight belt. Then she was grabbing at her own, letting it drop onto the sand beside the rope, and she felt herself turn buoyant again. He was pulling up through the water, and she was beside him, kicking her fins.... It was a race, clearly; she didn't have to be Jax to know that. They had to beat the copies to the top.

Those versions of themselves were not them. They were him.

And they could hurt Hayley.

Gasping, she and Jax broke the surface.

And there was Hayley, sitting in the kayak, looking shockingly normal—part of the world of makeup and clothes and TV, the regular, mundane world.

Her face was lit up by one of the flashlights; apparently she hadn't wanted to sit alone in the dark.

The boat was rocking a bit but not close to flipping.

"I can't believe it!" she said. "Wow, what a relief. I was about to call 911!"

But then, behind her on the other side of the boat, in the dark, another Jax and Cara broke the surface too. Hayley jumped in her seat and turned around, shining her flashlight down at them and giving a short shriek.

All of them pulled out their mouthpieces hastily, all four of them struggled to raise their masks onto their head so they could talk to Hayley. All four of them had bruise-like creases on their cheeks where the masks had bitten in.

"They're not us," Cara told her, her lips numb with cold.

"They're *him*," said Jax. "Don't believe them."

"No," said the fake Jax, talking just like the real one. "*We're* real. Those are the copies. Please, Hayley. Believe us."

"Please, Hayley," begged the fake Cara. "It's me!"

It was amazing how much she looked like her—even her voice, the way she ran her hand over her wet hair.

"You have to choose," said the fake Jax. "You have to choose between us. Choose the real ones. Choose *us*!"

The real Jax bobbed up and down in the water, splashing. "Hayley! Be careful! If you choose wrong they'll hurt you—"

"So choose right!" said the fake Cara. "Choose me!"

"Follow your instincts, Hayley," said Jax, shaking his head. "Don't second-guess yourself. You know the real us, I know you do."

Treading water, Cara gazed up at her friend, who was casting the beam of the flashlight back and forth between the two sets of them.

"What is this," said Hayley, sounding angry. "What's happening?"

"*You* are the arbiter," said the real Jax. "Not Max. It's you who's supposed to be the impartial judge. But you have to choose the version of us that's real, Hayley. That's real and wants to be good."

"I'm sorry for bringing you here," said Cara. "I am...but the bad one could say that too, the copy of me. But she couldn't know what's on your mother's shelf of statues, could she? She could never know that. Could she?"

"Careful," warned Jax. "If I know, the fake me could know, too. Because he can read me."

"I know what's beside the girl with the white goose," said Cara. "Do you?"

The real Jax shook his head.

"Hayley," urged Cara. "It's the gnome thing with the cone-shaped hat. And the basket of mushrooms. Could the copy know that?"

"Don't ask me," said Hayley.

Behind her, the false Cara smiled. "I know that too. She said it first, that's all. And I know more important things, also," she said. "I know how you feel about *Max*."

Cara groaned and looked over at Jax.

"No! Don't choose them! They're going to hurt you!"

Hayley was casting the flashlight back and forth between them. Cara couldn't see her face behind the brightness of the beam and felt panicked suddenly. It was too much to ask of Hayley, too much to ask of anyone.

"OK," said Hayley, and swung her light from one pair of them to the other. "I pick. It's *you*."

Who? Cara squinted up until the light was out of her eyes again. She saw Hayley looking down—at *her*.

The real her and the real Jax.

Cara let out a sigh of relief—and as she did so her friend swung the beam around again, till it pointed at the copies.

They were melting, their faces losing definition like wax statues under a flame. They flowed onto the top of the water, spreading like oil, and dispersed.

In a few seconds there was no trace at all.

There was a brief pause, full of the sound of her and Jax breathing.

"Nice," said Jax, when he had caught his breath.

"How did you know?" asked Cara.

"I didn't," said Hayley, and raised her shoulders in a quick shrug. "You guys just seemed more desperate...plus, I admit. I didn't think you'd throw the Max thing in my face."

"Does this mean he's gone?" Cara asked her brother.

"For now," he said.

Her heart sank. When would they beat him so he didn't come back at all?

"Listen," said Jax, and put his mask back on. "Our work's not quite done yet. Almost, but not quite. Hold on, OK, Hayley? Just a few more minutes. Dive down along the rope, Cara, and put your weights back on."

"We'll be back," said Cara, and slid in her regulator.

"No!" said Hayley. "Are you kidding? Don't you dare—"

But they had to, and following her little brother, Cara sank underneath the waves again.

⊰⊱

They were going down, down, down—pushing without the dive weights took far more effort—and Cara saw that the glow was starting to diminish. Whether the plankton were leaving or winking out she didn't know; there was still some brightness in the water, but it was definitely less.

As they neared the bottom she felt something fly past her—a flash of bubbles, glinting in the dimness.

On the soft sand of the bottom, Jax handed her her weight belt again. She clipped it around her waist and then thought, trying to pull at him: *Jax. What was that? Moving past us?*

He shook his head.

As they made their way toward where they'd met the selkie, Cara looked down and around at the wreck fragments poking out of the ground. It was harder to see now, with the light fading, and she had to concentrate hard to make out shapes through the growing gloom.

Where were the ghosts?

And then she saw—in the darkness beyond, she could detect their shapes, their eyes and their lips and thin hands. But then the shapes were changing. The outlines flickered and when they reappeared were different. The bodies turned sparkling, becoming less dark—they were all shining now, twinkling and glistening and fading.

What is it? What are they? she thought at Jax.

They're like dolphins, said Jax's clear head-voice. *But not exactly. I think it's—yeah. They're dolphins now, but they're also still ghosts. Ghosts that can leave this place, finally.*

And the translucent dolphins were churning the water, and then they leapt in a great, joyful rush, spinning past her and Jax and leaving streams of silver bubbles in their wake—passing them both in a kind of quick caress, a series of grateful nods good-bye.

Cara thought: So now they're free.

She watched as the wake of their bubbles vanished into the dim distance, and behind them the water settled into quietude once again.

After a long moment she felt a presence behind her, and she and Jax rotated slowly, swishing their swim-fins. The selkie was hovering, her dark eyes like pools you could fall into and never come out of.

But instead of giving them something—instead of handing over the key—she laid one of her flippers where Cara thought her heart might be. She bowed her head to both of them. And then, in a whirl of water, she too was gone.

Nine

When they got back to shore they were too tired to take the boat home with them, so instead of hitching it back onto the bike they hid it in the undergrowth to pick up later, along with the scuba gear and the snarled-up, peeled-off wetsuits. They were too tired to do almost anything but pull their sandy clothes on and start pedaling home; the sounds of dawn rose around them, birdsong and faint car noises, and light streaked through the sky, pink and yellow.

"So," said Hayley. "When do I, like, get the skinny on what happened back there?"

"There were—there were these ghosts underwater," said Cara wearily.

"Say what?"

"Dead," said Cara. "These ghosts that used to be the crew of the *Whydah*. Like, pirates."

"Cara had a faceoff with the Pouring Man," said Jax. "That was when he split into two and shifted his shape…."

"We had to win over the ghosts to our side," said Cara. "They were—Jax says they were the ghosts of the pirates from that ship. The pirates of the *Whydah*."

Hayley just looked at them over her handlebars, her mouth open.

"He tried to scare us. He's all about fear," said Cara, but it sounded stupid, and she lapsed into an exhausted silence.

She wanted to ask Jax what had happened, why, after all that, the selkie hadn't given them the key. At the same time, she wanted to tell him not to read her anymore, since the emergency was over. But of course she couldn't, not with Hayley here—Hay didn't know about Jax's ability, and it had to stay that way.

"Of course," said Jax suddenly. "I won't."

"Won't what?" asked Hayley.

"Don't worry about it," said Cara.

"And about the key," went on Jax. "We're covered."

"Later, when I'm not totally wiped out?" said Hayley. "I'm gonna need the 411."

They rode quietly again. They'd forgotten to take towels with them so their hair was still wet and full of salt, their fingers and toes were just coming out of numbness, and they shivered in the chill early morning air as they pedaled. Cara could barely keep her eyes open; her arms and legs ached, and she wondered if it was tiredness or some lingering pain from the Pouring Man's invading her.

"Uh-oh," said Jax as they cruised slowly down their street.

Hayley peeled off down her driveway; there was Lolly, waiting for them at their front door.

Her toddler grandson was holding on to her leg beside her, his face smeared with applesauce.

It was a good question, Cara thought, whether he or Lolly looked more disgusted with Jax and her.

"We're really sorry," said Cara humbly as they trudged up the steps.

"We're very sorry," agreed Jax, nodding.

Lolly seemed like she was about to yell at them. But then she must have noticed the state they were in, because her face softened a bit.

Maybe, thought Cara, she was deciding she had priorities other than yelling.

She shook her head, turned, and disappeared down the hall, and they followed her in. When she came back she was carrying plush bath towels that were still warm from the dryer.

Gratefully, Cara took one. As she rubbed her wet hair with it she realized the exhaustion she felt wasn't necessarily bad; it was a sweet tiredness. It had a sense of accomplishment. She saw the dolphins' glittering trails as they moved up through the water toward the surface, toward sunlight, and knew she and Jax had actually *done* something.

She'd been happy plenty of times in her life, but she couldn't remember feeling glad like this.

"Both of you: hot showers. Right away. You, Jax, downstairs. Cara, you take the upstairs bathroom. Meanwhile, I'll make oatmeal. Brown sugar and cinnamon. Your lips are blue! As if your poor father doesn't have enough to worry about with Max laid up in the hospital and the family car crumpled up like an accordion! He'll be home in less than half an hour. You hear me? He just called. I didn't say anything about all this, because thankfully I hadn't checked your rooms yet. If I'd known you'd disappeared I would have ended up scaring the bejaysus out of that man for absolutely no reason. He's in a cab from the ferry dock right now. Headed for the rental-car place to pick up a car to use, then home, then to the hospital. And you should both go with him. Half an hour at the most! I want you warm and dry before then. And sitting at the table for breakfast. Go! Now!"

All Cara wanted to do was sleep, but as Lolly grabbed Jax by the elbow and steered into the nearby bathroom she headed up the stairs to immerse herself—this time in water that was not freezing and not salty, not home to the Pouring Man and not shining with billions of microorganisms.

❖

At the hospital, they left their dad sitting next to Max's bed, patting the hand that wasn't in the cast. Max was too big and tough for hand-holding these days and looked pretty close to his old self to Cara—not upset or in pain or anything, just bored of the hospital room and restless to be released.

Still, it was pretty obvious that her dad, who felt so bad about not being there when it happened, wanted time alone with him; the story of what had happened last night would have to wait till later. So she and Jax closed the door behind them and took the elevator down to the cafeteria.

It smelled like processed cheese food mixed with plastic. They lined up and pushed their trays along the metal rails, each grabbing a small plate with pudding and a whorled flower of whipped cream on it. Apparently it was the only dessert that was served here, at least in the morning.

Then they found a table near a big window, where they could see into the tops of the trees outside.

"So tell me," said Cara. "You said it was OK, about the key. I mean—did she tell you where it was or something? What did she tell you?"

Jax spooned up pudding, smearing it on his mouth and chin. Not unlike Lolly's grandson, who was two.

Telepath. Genius. Slob.

"The key," he said, with his mouth full, "isn't a physical object. The key is something we have to do."

"It's *always* something we have to do!" burst out Cara, exasperated.

She'd been hoping the key would be real—i.e., an actual *key*. A key to a locker or a box or a chest that would give them what they needed to get their mother back.

A key to buried treasure, she realized, basically.

Was that too much to ask?

So maybe it would have been too good to be true. But part of her had still hoped.

"I know," said Jax.

"And actually? I don't really need to see your food while you're eating it," said Cara.

"Huh," said Jax, chewing. "Well, you're the one who asked me to talk."

"It just—it seems like whatever we do, the next step is to do something else. Find the leatherback. Solve the poem. See the tide. Meet the selkie. Free the ghosts. *Fight the fear!*"

"What'd you expect? I mean there's a reason they call them *quests*. It's not like sitting on your butt and watching TiVo," said Jax, and pushed away his empty plate.

"You have an answer for everything, don't you?" said Cara.

"Hey, it's who I am," said Jax. "What can I say."

"So, spill it. What do we have to do?"

"It's kind of this—ritual, I guess," said Jax.

"Yeah? And what's the point of it?"

She was in a bad mood, suddenly. When they got back from undersea she'd been almost euphoric, but now she felt let down.

"It's just fatigue," said Jax.

She hadn't anything out loud. She felt spied on.

"You're not supposed to do that!" she snapped.

"I didn't do anything!" protested Jax. "You had a look on your face! I just reacted to it, like anybody else!"

She clicked her tongue and shook her head, not quite sure if she believed him.

"Whatever," she said finally, and looked away, drumming her fingers on the smooth top of the cafeteria table.

"The ceremony," he went on, "has to be done tonight. Well, first thing tomorrow morning, I guess—right after midnight, that is."

She groaned.

"Are we allowed to sleep? *Ever?*"

"Hey man, we'll sleep when we're dead," came a voice from behind them.

Max was rolling up to the table in a wheelchair, pushed by a nurse, with their dad a few feet behind him.

Cara thought it must be a line from a song.

"Geez," said Jax. "Is something wrong with your legs, too?"

"They always make you leave in a wheelchair, even if you can walk," said Max.

"Standard policy," said the nurse, nodding.

"That's Kafkaesque," said Jax in an admiring tone.

"Cough-what?" said Max.

"You kids ready?" asked their dad.

He looked pale, Cara thought. Even more so than she'd become used to, over the course of the summer. Hadn't he been outside at all? In all the months of the summer, hadn't he seen the sun?

He'd been in his office, she thought. In his study where he worked—and even slept, on that narrow sofa.

She felt a rush of concern for her dad. Was he actually doing worse than any of them?

She reached out and squeezed his hand. He looked down at her and smiled as he squeezed back—grateful, she thought.

They followed Max, and the nurse who was pushing him, out through the hospital's automatic front doors. Walking behind the nurse, Cara wondered why they always wore the same shoes, white and homely with big thick soles.

Maybe it was a nursing rule—like good-looking, normal-colored shoes would make people sicker.

"I'll bring the rental car around," said their dad. "You three wait here."

"You can get out now, sweetcheeks," said the nurse to Max, and Cara watched as she rumpled his hair with her pink-nailed hand.

Apparently even fifty-year-old ladies had crushes on her brother.

The nurse went inside again, taking the wheelchair with her.

"*Sweetcheeks!*" said Jax.

The three of them watched their dad hurry across the parking lot, dangling his keys from one hand. Then Max elbowed Cara with his good arm.

"I miss anything?"

She and Jax looked at each other and smiled.

"You could say that," she said.

"We did it," said Jax—a certain satisfaction in his voice, Cara thought. His chest was sticking out a bit, too. "We went down to the *Whydah*."

Max's mouth gaped open, making him look not so bright.

"You—what? No way!"

"Way," said Jax, smugly.

"But how?"

"We used the scuba gear," said Cara, and shrugged. She couldn't help feeling a little smug herself. "It worked."

"Man," said Max bitterly, and shook his head. "I can't believe I missed it."

"We're sorry, too," said Jax, and Cara thought he actually looked sincere. Max had really been into the pirate-ship thing, that was true. He had to be disappointed.

"We had to go," said Cara. "You know that, right? We saw the light on the ocean. It was time. We couldn't wait."

Max kept shaking his head—he could barely believe it had happened without him, she thought.

"We missed you being there," said Cara. "Actually, I was…well. I was terrified. I didn't want to go without you. I almost called. But then I thought of you, you know, here." She gestured at the hospital behind them. "And I didn't think it would be fair to wake you up when there was no way you could leave your bed anyway."

"I guess," said Max after a second, gruffly.

"As far as the actual ship went," said Jax, "there wasn't much left to see. Just sand, mostly. Some ancient rotted timbers. You know: they'd already brought up the treasure."

"OK, spill it," said Max reluctantly. "Quick, before Dad gets back."

So they told him the story, falling over each other a bit to get to the most amazing parts—the selkie, the pirates with their translucence and their impossibility. When Cara described how the ghosts had been set free, he looked almost suspicious—as though that detail was more astounding than an encounter with a half-seal, half-human out of Celtic mythology.

She wished she could have taken a picture for him.

They were still talking excitedly when a horn honked and they looked up to see an unfamiliar vehicle pull up—a bright-red convertible sports car, with their dad driving.

"It was all they had," he said sheepishly.

"A Camaro? You look like one of those midlife-crisis guys," said Max cheerily, and got into the front.

The car only had two doors, so Cara and Jax jumped over the side into the squished backseat.

"Thanks a lot, Maximilian," said their dad. He pushed a button, and the top started moving up, closing over their heads.

"Does it go fast?" asked Jax, as they buckled their belts.

The car pulled away from the curb—hesitantly.

"Your brother just totaled the car. You want to know if he can total this one, too?" asked their dad.

"It wasn't his fault," said Jax. Cara shot him a look, worried he might say too much.

"The deer," said their dad, and nodded. "I know. It could happen to anyone. But there was no deer on the scene, according to the police. Right? He never hit it. You swerved, didn't you, Max."

"Swerved, yeah," said Max. "So I, uh, wouldn't hit the deer."

"Deer sighting or not, it's not going to look good to our insurance company. Believe you me."

"He's in the dreaded under-25 male driver bracket,"

said Jax to Cara, nodding sagely. "They wreck everything. It costs the earth to insure them."

"You got me into this," said Max testily.

"Got you into what?" asked their dad.

There was an awkward silence.

"Oh, I—I made him go out in the car just then," said Jax. "I wanted a bear claw."

Their dad looked at them in the rearview mirror—it was a thin explanation, and Cara could tell he didn't buy it.

Still, in for a penny, in for a pound, as her dad liked to say.

"He was whining, so Max just said, you know, give me a break, I'll get you your stupid donut," she elaborated. "You know how they have them at the general store sometimes, and Jax didn't want to walk."

"Huh," said their dad.

The silence started up again.

"Sorry, everyone," said Jax, and leaned up to pat Max on the shoulder.

"Yeah, well," said Max.

"Look, guys," said their dad. "Sure, maybe I shouldn't have gone. It's tough that you had to be without me after everything that's happened this summer…"

They came off a fast roundabout and merged onto Route 6. Cars rushed by, overtaking each other and whipping past, and Cara thought how lucky Max had been, in the end. How lucky they all were. She remembered how their car had looked last time she saw it, wrapped around the tree like the tree was a part of it.

Their dad was going to get another shock when he saw the car.

"…and I think maybe part of me was hoping that by going away, even for just two days, I might—I might return to find something had changed. Or more precisely, that things had returned to the way they used to be. In other words…that your mother would magically *be* here when I got back."

Cara shot a quick look at Jax and saw that, like Max, he was studiously staring out his window. All of a sudden things were very interesting outside all the windows, in fact.

"And it impaired my judgment. You could have been hurt far worse than you were, Max, and that would have been partly my fault."

"Come on," said Max after a moment. "Don't make this so global, Dad. You didn't do anything wrong. You went to a conference, I got in a fender-bender. Accidents just happen."

"If that's a fender-bender, I'd like to see a head-on collision," muttered Jax under his breath, but luckily their dad was still talking and didn't hear.

"…but I'm afraid you've got to take responsibility, too," said their father. "You weren't authorized to take the car out, Max, except for emergencies and to pick me up at the ferry. I was perfectly clear there. You knew that."

"Yeah," said Max. "But—"

"No buts," said their father. "I'm sorry about your arm, I really am. But I'm also going to have to ground you. Until school starts."

They were silent. Max was the one who'd gotten hurt—he'd gotten hurt for all of them. And now he was grounded.

It wasn't fair at all, thought Cara.

Max wasn't saying anything, and she couldn't see his face to know how pissed off he was.

The radio droned.

"...for the first time in human history, the Arctic could be ice-free as early as within the next few years—meaning mass drownings for polar bears...."

Listening to it, her dad shook his head.

"Will they cover a new car for us, at least?" asked Max. "I mean, I get that the premiums will go up. And that really sucks. But will we get a new car soon?"

"As far as I know," said their dad, preoccupied.

"I'd feel bad," said Max—trying to inject some levity, Cara thought—"if you, like, had to hitchhike to teach next week."

Her dad shushed them and turned the radio volume up. "This is the stuff your mother is working on," he said.

"Global warming, right?" said Max. "The paranoid left-wing conspiracy that doesn't really exist."

Their dad looked at him sharply, then saw he was kidding.

"Left-wing, right-wing, rubbish," said their father. "It's a little thing called science."

"Actually," said Jax, "technically she's working on ocean acidification, which is related to climate change via the CO_2 connection but not the same phenomenon."

"So, this weekend," said their dad, once the news turned to sports, "we all need to sit down and have a talk about what's going to happen this fall, how things will work with just the four of us, and how we're going to deal with the problem of your mother being missing. Going forward. We need to talk it through. OK?"

Cara raised her eyebrows; Jax shot her another sidelong look.

"And we'll pick up a pizza from Red Barn and watch a movie afterward," added their dad, as if to lessen the blow.

"Sure, Dad," answered Max, their delegate to the older generation. "We'll talk."

❧

"I wonder if Hayley should be here," said Max.

It was the quietest hour of sunset, the sky a dim pastel-colored wash of fading colors over the trees and the water of the bay silvery-black and lapping at the shore. Faintly they could smell barbeque smoke from down the street and hear the sound of mosquitoes hitting the neighbor's blue-light bug zapper.

They'd eaten dinner early and were sitting on the porch, swinging back and forth. Their dad, who seemed to have given them a free pass on chores for the day, was inside tidying up with Lolly. He'd said that after that was done he'd do some pruning in the back before it got dark; gardening took his mind off things, Cara suspected.

"I mean, didn't you say she turned out to play the role of the arbiter, or whatever I was supposed to be? So maybe she should be here for the ritual too," Max went on.

"I talked to her earlier," said Cara. "Her mom's not letting her come over for a while. She's mad because Hayley showed up all exhausted and dirty from the sleepover and wouldn't admit we did anything, you know, out of the ordinary. She didn't want us to get in trouble, so she just said we stayed up late talking. But then she collapsed and slept, like, forever. All day, up until an hour ago. So anyway, her mom's making her work at the salon till further notice."

"So," said Max. "We need to prepare, I guess."

Jax nodded. "There are some things we need. We need salt, for example. It should be sea salt, ideally."

"I think there's some in the kitchen," said Cara.

"Then we each need something of Mom's. It could be even hair, from her hairbrush. I got the feeling it should basically be something that has her DNA. Or something a dog would use to track her scent, you know? Though I couldn't exactly swear to that."

"Creepy," said Max. "Eye of newt, or whatever."

"Huh?" asked Jax.

"Wow, something you don't know," Max marveled. "We had to read it in English this year. *Macbeth.* The play by Shakespeare? There's witches in it, and they have this recipe for a potion, I think: eye of newt, toe of frog. Then something else I forget. Wait, maybe the hair of the dog...?"

"The point of the whole deal," said Jax, "is it's a warding spell, basically. When we do the ritual, we make her safe from him. At least, for a while. More than that, I don't know."

"So what else?" asked Cara.

"There are a couple of herbs I think we have in the kitchen. Apparently they're ancient. People have used them for centuries even though you can pick them up for $1.99 at Stop & Shop."

"Who knew," said Max, deadpan.

The sprinkler started up in front of them, going back and forth in the humid, dusky air. Its movement was hypnotic and oddly calming.

"No, really," said Jax. "The selkie told me there are things all around with these properties. These properties that seem to defy physics, defy chemistry. And some of the things with extraordinary properties are totally basic-seeming—even trivial. You'd never think they were anything more than that. Unless you knew. Unless you had this secret, ancient knowledge. It used to be passed down by word of mouth, between generations of—shamans, I guess she called them? But now that tradition has died out. It's all, I don't know, TV and advertising and selling things and the old secrets have been lost."

"To all but the seal people," said Max, a bit mockingly.

Max could mock, but Cara didn't mind. She knew with perfect certainty about the world that was hidden—knew it was there, though she didn't understand it. So Max could mock, but she didn't mind. The mockery had no teeth.

"Not seal people, exactly," said Jax, and was going to explain, but Cara stopped him.

"We should focus," she said. "We don't have that long for the gathering. Tell us what else we'll need."

The sprinkler, which had started low, had gotten taller until the lines of spray were falling down on the roof of the porch as it passed them.

"Dad," called out Max, craning his neck around the corner of the house, "you made the sprinkler too big. Can you cut it down? We're about to get wet here."

"But I didn't turn the sprinkler on," their dad called back. He was clearly still in the kitchen.

Cara looked at Jax. In that second of recognition—Cara thinking *Oh, not again. How stupid can I be?*—the lines of water coming out of the sprinkler shot up into the sky suddenly, as though the water pressure had hit infinity.

At the same time the water turned color—turned dark red, red as blood. Then it was pouring down on the roof, hitting the roof of the porch so hard it leaked through the cracks above them, flowing down over the sides in thin curtains of red.

"Inside!" Cara screamed, and all three of them piled through the front door. She slammed it behind them, and they stood there breathing hard.

From the kitchen, Lolly called out a question—what was going on, or something. Before they could answer, or even pay attention, Max said: "*Rufus.*"

He had been beside them on the porch, curled up on the wooden slats as they swung.

"Oh *no*," said Cara.

How could they have left him behind?

"I'll get him!" said Max, and before they could stop him he had opened the door and was through it.

"Don't bring him in!" yelled Jax, but it was too late: there was Rufus, Max holding him by the collar with his good hand, the arm in the cast hanging limp; the dog was soaked, soaked in the blood-red water.

"Oh. No," said Cara again.

"Max, you don't get it," urged Jax. "You have to get him out of the house! Now!"

Rufus growled.

And Cara knew it, she knew it instantly.

He wasn't their Rufus anymore. He was *inhabited*.

"Max invited him," said Jax. "Now he's in."

And then Rufus smiled.

It was far worse than the growling. It was one of the most frightening things Cara had ever seen.

It was like his lips were being formed into a grin by some force beyond him—a manipulation, a form of cold, ugly puppetry.

"Jesus!" said Max as the dog swiveled its head and looked at him. He snatched his hand off the collar as though it was hot to the touch.

"Get him out!" cried Jax.

Cara grabbed a coat and threw it over the dog's head, his teeth snapping, head thrusting up and down. She backed him up toward the door as Max wrenched it open, and then they had him out again and the door slammed behind him.

"What were you *doing* to that poor dog, for Chrissake?" asked their dad, sounding angry. He stood in the doorway to the kitchen, holding a dishtowel.

He'd never been able to stand it when people mistreated animals.

"He was—" began Jax.

"We think he got skunked," rushed Max. "Maybe right in the face? He was bringing it in."

"I don't smell anything," said their dad.

"That's because of Cara's quick thinking, then," said Max.

"Huh," said their dad. "Well, if he was really skunked you'll need the special soap. It's still under the basement sink from last time. I'll let the three of you deal with it."

"Will do," said Max.

"And don't bring him inside, whatever you do," he added before retreating again.

"He's right about that part," whispered Jax. "When the water dries off Roof, or isn't in him anymore, he should revert. I *hope*. But for sure we can't go near him, at least until then."

"Whew," said Max. "So that was the guy I saw? He can do that? Horrorshow."

They sat down on the bottom stairs of the staircase, all three of them in a row. Cara thought the sound of the sprinkler had stopped, but she wasn't sure. They could hear a faint but steady scratching at the door. She wondered if any of the neighbors had come outside, had watched the blood-red water shoot up into the sky and rain down on their house in a torrent.

They'd get some weird looks tomorrow if the neighbors had noticed. That was for sure.

"Wait him out," said Jax. "It's all we can do."

"But what about the warding charm?" asked Cara. "What if it's not dry outside by then?"

"We're lucky on that one," said Jax. "Except for the Rufus factor, that is. The path of the ritual is from the back of the house, the basement door, right down to the water. The front yard's not part of it."

"But he could attack, couldn't he?" said Max. "If he still has…that…inside him."

"Probably someone should leash him," said Cara. "We should tie him up. Shouldn't we? I mean it's not only us—he could hurt someone else, with the Pouring Man telling him what to do. And then poor old Roof would be blamed. And none of this is his fault."

"But it's too dangerous," said Jax.

"I'll do it," said Max.

"With a broken arm? Great idea," said Cara.

"I'll do it," Max insisted. "I can still use my fingers a bit. It's not like the hand is completely useless. Enough to snap the leash anyway."

Before they could stop him, Max had grabbed the leash from its coat hook and was outside. The door closed behind him.

"That's just great," said Jax. "What if the man gets in *him,* too? *Then* what? Because he wasn't with us last night, he isn't as safe as we are. He's got no protection."

"You have to tell him that," said Cara. "*We* do."

They expected sounds of growling and biting outside, but none came. Cara felt nervous. It was too quiet.

"I have to see," she said, and opened the door a crack to peer out.

At the end of the porch Max was lying facedown, turned away. Rufus was leashed to the rail—but he was also hunched over Max, gnawing.

Gnawing.

"Max!" she cried, and without another thought she jumped out and was on him. The dog was growling and snapping, but she didn't care—she dove past him, grabbed Max and dragged him, and then he rolled over and was crawling, too, and they were at the door and the dog was biting at their shoes, had one of Cara's shoes off and pulled it right off her foot so that her sock-foot dragged across the porch slats.... She felt the dog's wet mouth on her ankle and a pang of fear, but then Jax was there and they were in.

Jax slammed the door closed again.

Breathing hard, she grabbed Max's shoulder.

"Max! Where'd he bite you?" she asked.

Max rubbed his eyes and then raised his broken arm weakly. Halfway between the elbow and the wrist the cast was almost gnawed through, with a gouge in it that was nothing but a pulpy, dirty mass of plaster and gauze.

There was something on it that looked like blood, red smudges and smears, but she realized it wasn't Max's blood. It was the red water soaking Rufus's fur.

The not-dog's teeth hadn't reached Max's skin.

They lay there, recovering.

"Children?" called Lolly. "What's all the ruckus about? Are you playing too rough out there?"

Rolled eyes.

"Just—uh, just *playing* normal!" called Jax. "Sorry! We'll try to be quieter."

They waited for a second, making sure she wasn't coming out into the hallway.

"Thanks, Car," got out Max finally. "He faked me out. He let me clip him, and then he knocked me down. I held him off with the cast, but—"

"How does it feel?" asked Jax.

"It's OK, I think. A little sore. I'll have to get it fixed—"

"Max, listen," said Cara. "You can't take on the Pouring Man. What we did last night? It gave us some protection from him. Facing him down, I mean. But you don't have that protection. So you have to be really careful of him."

"Promise, Max?" asked Jax. "Let us take the risks."

Max just groaned, a groan of frustration. Or annoyance.

Then he said, "I totally remembered, by the way."

"Remembered what?" asked Cara.

"What the witches said. We had to memorize it. 'Eye of newt and toe of frog, wool of bat and tongue of dog. Adder's fork, and blind-worm's sting, lizard's leg and howlet's wing.'"

"What's a howlet?" asked Cara.

"No idea."

"Probably an archaic form of *owl*," said Jax. "Luckily, we don't have to dissect anything for this particular charm."

"Thank the lord for small mercies," said Max.

Ten

"There isn't any incantation," whispered Jax. *"Nothing for us* to say but Mom's name. There *is* something I have to *think*— that is, hold in my mind, is what the selkie said—at a certain point while we're casting the herbs on the ground. Part of a rune poem in an ancient language. Something about the North Star. I think it means, more or less, 'The star keeps faith with us, never failing, always on its course through the mists of the night.'"

"Uh, right," said Max.

"Say it how it really sounds," said Cara, curious.

"Tir biþ tacna sum, healdeð trywa wel wiþ æþelingas; a biþ on færylde ofer nihta genipu, næfre swiceþ," recited Jax.

It sounded very strange—as though Jax was speaking in tongues, which Cara had seen once in a horror movie Max forced them to watch that involved snake-handling.

"So, nothing to, like, chant?" asked Max. "No toil and trouble?"

"You're off the hook," said Jax.

The three of them were huddled just inside the back door that led outside from the kitchen, down a narrow gravel path through their small backyard and beneath the pitch pines to the water. Their dad had gone to sleep in his own bed, instead of on the couch in his office, for once, so he was two floors up, and—they hoped—wouldn't be able to hear them.

"Once we make the salt lines and cast the charm, each of us stands in position. You have the positions, right? Everyone's clear on that?"

As soon as it was midnight they had to draw three lines in salt, one from the back door and two from the back corners of the house, all the way down to the water. Then they had to walk along those lines and sprinkle herbs they carried in china bowls—part of an herbal charm, Jax called it, that included dried seasonings from their mother's spice cabinet, things like thyme and fennel. It was part of a "tenth-century Anglo-Saxon charm," according to Jax, passed along to the selkie by someone else, and that was all Cara had taken in.

The selkie was a messenger, Jax said.

Cara felt nervous. Her palms were sweating.

"Jax," she whispered when Max stepped back into the kitchen for a second to glug down some water. "You can ping me, during this, OK? But only till the minute it's over. If you need to."

"OK," whispered Jax solemnly. "Thanks."

"Each of us holds their talisman," said Max, back again. "In the right hand and tied with a white string around the right wrist. Check?"

"Check," whispered Cara.

She had one of her mother's lipsticks, Max had a small jeweled comb, and Jax had a bracelet with their mother's name spelled out on it, from when she was younger.

"Check," said Max.

"So after we draw the lines and sprinkle the herbs, we take up our positions. At the door and corners. And we wait there for nine minutes with our eyes closed, then open them and wait for another three. Closed for nine, open for three, got it? Nine and three are significant numbers in the charm, for some reason. And no talking during *any* of this. Silence is as important to the ritual as any words would be. Got that? A single word could *wreck* it."

"We got it, J," said Max.

"Watches all say 11:57:24?"

"Yes," said Cara.

She didn't have a digital watch. She thought they were hideous and always checked the time on her cell, but she'd borrowed an old one of her dad's.

"Here, too," said Max.

"How did they time this whole ritual thing before there were watches?" wondered Cara.

"Probably counting, and I bet it took a lot of practice and discipline," said Jax. "So we have it easy. And Max, your watch is set so you can punch in the alarm for nine minutes, right? So we know when to open our eyes?"

"Done deal."

"At that point, when the whole twelve minutes are up, the warding charm is finished. The protection part of the rite. The rest is to make her welcome, or something. So we walk from our stations down to the water again, along those same lines of power where the salt is. And we all meet at the point where the salt lines converge. Right down there at the shore. We kneel and dip our foreheads in the water. We touch our right hands to our heart, with the talismans in them. And we say her name. Can you guys remember all that?"

"We'll manage," said Max.

"Then it's back to the house, but this time face away from the sea. Stand still. Heads bowed. Don't move. Just wait. If we've done it right, after a while we'll get a sign."

"Oh," said Cara, "and we can't forget to put this near the waterline."

She'd brought one of her mother's light, cotton sundresses, flung over a shoulder, because the selkie had said: *her clothes.* The instructions had said to place her clothes near the water and hold the talismans.

"OK," said Jax.

"We all have our salt," said Cara.

"We have to start walking and sprinkling the salt exactly at the stroke of midnight, remember," said Jax.

"On my mark," said Max. "I'll say go."

The moon was still hidden, so the only lights they had to walk by were the lights of their headlamps. With all the things they had to have in their hands for the ritual, there was no way they could also carry flashlights. Which made the headlamps necessary. Max had said that wearing his made him feel like a coal miner. Or a spelunker, Jax had added, and then had to explain to them that that meant *explorer of caves.*

Cara looked down and checked: salt and herbs in her left hand, lipstick in her right palm and tied around that same wrist with string. She still had to hold it, since there was no surefire way to secure the shiny metal cylinder by tying it.

"Go," hissed Max, and Cara pushed the back door open. They went through single-file, shifted their salt shakers into the hands holding the talismans while their left hands held the herb bowls, and started walking and sprinkling the salt on the ground.

As they had planned, each of them struck out in a precise direction—Cara straight down toward the water, Max to the right corner of the house, Jax to the left.

Cara bent her head and aimed her headlamp at her feet, because if she tripped on the dark grass the salt or the herbs could go flying—one misstep could ruin the whole ceremony, Jax had warned. She held her breath. Her fingers shook as she tipped the salt shaker back and forth. The trees loomed up in front of her, and she was making her way through them—walking as straight as she could, slow and deliberate so as not to drop anything.... Slowly the waterline drew near.

A few feet away from it she bent and let the sundress fall into a heap, then kept walking. Just as she began sinking into the mud, the water lapping at her toes, she stopped and let the last of her salt drift down into the mud.

"Oh no!" came Jax's voice plaintively from close by, somewhere in the marshy area before the trees started up.

"I'm out of salt! And I'm not down at the water yet! It must have come out of my shaker too fast!"

It's my fault, thought Cara. They hadn't had three salt shakers in the house, so for one of them she'd had to use a cinnamon container, and she recalled, now, how large the holes had been in the plastic lid for the cinnamon. She'd made a note to warn the others, and then, when they were distributing the different containers, she'd completely forgotten to mention it.

I'm sorry, it's my fault, she thought again—more loudly, if that was possible. She tried to send the thought in Jax's direction, so he didn't feel like it was him who'd messed up.

"Keep going anyway," came Max's confident voice from her other side. "Just keep going. That'll be a gap in the line of defense, but we can work around it. We'll have to."

She saw Jax come down to the water, stuffing the empty shaker into his pocket.

Then they were all side by side at the waterline, at the convergence. They stood there awkwardly for a moment—Cara felt foolish; it was hard to believe anything real would come of this—then turned and began the walk back up, curving apart again as the salt lines separated. This time they were dropping herbs out of the bowls, pinch by pinch, which they lifted with their right thumb and forefinger. Cara retraced her steps back up to the house.

In a few seconds they were through the trees again and flattening their backs against the building's back wall, standing at their stations. Cara's station was the back door, where they'd all started out, and as she stood there with her eyes closed, everything went awfully silent—not even, she thought, the sound of a cricket. She stood in the blackness of her closed eyelids, feeling dizzy. Seeing the world kept you stable, she thought.

Then she heard the low growl of a dog.

It was Rufus—up front still, because the growl was very faint. In her whole life she'd never heard Rufus growl.

It must mean he wasn't himself again. Yet.

But she kept her eyes closed. She couldn't open them—it would ruin the ceremony. They had to be closed for the whole nine minutes, and she had to stand stock-still for those nine minutes too. No movement was allowed.

Fuzzy sparks pricked the inside of her eyelids—no problem, she told herself, that's just electrical impulses, isn't it? She tried to think what Jax would say: the science of it. It's what always happens when you keep your eyes closed for a long time without sleeping. There's no perfect black; there have to be interruptions in the blackness. So you imagine the sparks are pictures of things, images, while really it's neurons firing or whatever—the energy of the brain.

But then a picture was forming, a detailed picture with millions of tiny parts…impossible, yet crystal-clear. Like HD. She saw the front of the house; the light on the front porch must be on, because it was bright enough to see every speck of dust, every hair—she saw the peeling paint on the rail. She could tell it was night, though, from the way dark invaded from the corners….

Rufus was there, colored blood-red, his wet fur still dripping. He had sharp teeth and black eyes—the Pouring Man using the body of Rufus, using Rufus's poor, faithful old dog face, tail, dog legs.

The not-Rufus was worrying the leash, biting it where it was lashed to the white porch rails with their peeling, faded paint. The sharp teeth made a sawing sound on the nylon strap: saw. Saw. Saw.

She saw the not-dog's feet, with nails that were long and black and sharp. Not his real nails at all—these were claws like talons, scraping at the wood of the porch.

And then it happened. The leash broke—just as she heard the electronic beep of Max's watch alarm. And her eyes snapped open.

She realized she was gripping the lipstick so hard it was hurting her fingers.

Three more minutes till the warding charm was finished....he might be coming around the corner right now. His teeth, his needle-sharp teeth—not like her poor, sweet old Rufus at all. And they wouldn't be able to see him in the dark...she turned so that her headlamp swept the right-hand corner of the house, where Max stood. He must have turned to her at the same time, though, because she was blinded by the light from his headlamp and had to turn away. Then she looked left, to where Jax stood.

She thought: *Did you see it, too? Did you see the leash break?*

Jax reached up and clicked off his headlamp. She saw the beam wink off. Then he turned to her and shook his head.

No. She was the only one who'd seen it.

Then Max's watch alarm beeped again.

"Man!" said Max. "We can talk now, right, J? Was that a walk in the park, or what?"

"Be careful," she said to Max. "I think it's gotten loose! The dog-thing. And Jax and I are protected from him, I guess?—more than you, anyway, so watch out. He can still get at you. Because you're not—"

And that was when the not-dog came walking around the corner of the house. Not running; just walking.

Their headlamps illuminated him.

He was walking slowly, placidly.

And smiling as no dog ever should.

Showing long, needle-like teeth.

"He can't get through the salt line," said Jax in a rush. "So let's just keep going. Down to the water. We still have to do the welcoming part of the charm, or she won't be able to come home."

They started walking, turning every so often to see what the not-dog was doing. He kept walking parallel to them, down toward the water, outside the farthest salt line. He was on Max's side, not Jax's, at least, which meant he'd have to go around to get in where the gap was.

It'll be up to us to stop him, thought Jax at Cara as they walked. They weren't allowed to run—there was a measured pace to everything, a kind of dignity that had to be observed. *Even if his arm weren't broken, Max couldn't. He's too vulnerable. So if he goes around—if he tries to get in—we have to make a wall. You and me.*

Cara thought *Yes. OK.*

Max had already taken enough of a beating.

"Don't let him distract us from the ritual," called Max. "It's what he wants. Even I can see that, and that's without any ESP. At least, that I know of."

"Be careful, Max," said Jax. "OK? Be really careful."

Here they were, in the marsh flat again, the mud beneath their feet. Reeds tickled her shins.

"On our knees," said Max as they came together. "Foreheads in the water. And her name."

Cara felt her knees sinking into the mud, and out there somewhere she heard the not-dog splashing in the bay. Maybe he was already going around, trying to get to them. The top of her face was wet as she bent over, her hair dripping into her eyes. She squeezed the lipstick tight and held it to her chest, where she thought her heart was—in the middle and kind of to the left.

"Lily," said Max. At the same time Jax said "Mother" and Cara said "Mom" and thought: *Come home.*

"Here he is," said Jax, and they looked up from their kneeling positions to see the not-dog swimming in front of them. Swimming across the water a few feet out, in line with the shore…toward the place, on the other side of Jax, where there was a hole in the salt line. And no protection.

She felt the coldness in her again, not his deadly cold but the coldness of being afraid, and having to prepare. Still she braced herself, and she knew Jax was doing the same. He was getting ready.

They rose, backing away toward the salt-line gap, keeping their eyes and their headlamps on the not-dog, who was still paddling past them…keeping their eyes on the water.

What would they do? How could they keep him off Max, out of the safe place they'd made for their mother?

She didn't know. She felt the confusion of panic and reached out with her mind to Jax—

But then, behind the not-dog, something rose out of the waves. It was dark and light, both black and white and impossibly huge. She'd never seen anything that big rise out of the water—how it could even be here, in these muddy shallows, was a mystery…

It was an orca. A killer whale. Its teeth shone white in the light of their lamps as its great head reared out of the water of the bay. It rose above the not-dog, and the not-dog didn't even have time to bark.

"No!" Cara heard herself scream—because inside the not-dog was Rufus—it was Rufus, whom they had all loved for as long as she could remember—

The orca went higher and higher, an arc of water following it, a screen of water splashing out into the air—

And Max was screaming, too, and Jax—

But it was over in a second.

225

The not-dog was in the orca's teeth, and the orca sank back and was submerged again. There was not even a ripple where the orca had been.

Rufus was gone.

No one said anything for a while. They were done, she guessed—nothing left but to walk back up to the house. He was gone, anyway. And there was not a thing they could do about it.

Stunned, hanging their heads, they walked, defeated, back up through the reeds, through the trees, across the back lawn.

"Was that a—?" asked Max.

"*Orcinus orca*," said Jax. "Killer whale, or more rarely blackfish. Sometimes also called the seawolf."

"Do we even *have* those around here?"

"Not in three feet of water," said Jax quietly.

They took up their positions, their faces to the wall of the house. Cara felt tears streaming down her cheeks as she stood there. It was her fault. All of this. Her poor, dear dog.

The stupid cinnamon shaker. It was a tiny detail—a tiny, minuscule thing. The size of the holes in the shaker had gotten Rufus killed.

Her fault.

"No, honey," said someone behind her. "It's not your fault at all."

She knew the voice, of course.

But she didn't believe it. She was almost afraid to turn.

She did, finally. Slowly. Still clutching the lipstick.

And so did Jax, and Max. Cara was vaguely aware of them, off to the sides along the house's back wall....

The spot of Cara's headlamp trembled and then stood still. There she was. Their mother.

The same as ever, though maybe more tired-looking.

Her dark hair was stuck to the sides of her head, soaking wet and trailed back over her shoulders; she was barefoot and wore only the sundress Cara had brought.

She blinked in the glare and raised a hand to shade her eyes from the brightness of their headlamps.

Then they were running and piling onto her, their arms around her. Yelling, practically.

"Shh," she said, though maybe she was tearing up a little too, Cara thought, under the wide smile. "You'll wake up your father!"

"Who cares?" crowed Max.

"The thing is"—and their mother spoke softly, her arms still around them—"I'm afraid we'll have to let him sleep, this time."

They stepped back, looking at her—at least Cara and Max did. Jax was still clinging, his arms around her waist. She kept one arm around him, too.

They all took their headlamps off; Max reached up and hung his on a tree branch. It lit the yard around them.

"What do you mean?"

"I can't stay, darlings," she said, almost wincing. It was as if it hurt her just to say it.

"You can't *what?*"

Max took another step back.

"I know, Max," she said, nodding. "I know. It seems so wrong. To me, too."

"Tell us what's going on," said Cara.

"I can't tell you all of it. Not yet. But this is something we're all a part of, something we all have to do. It's what I told you when I came in the night, Cara."

"And what was that," said Max, almost coldly.

"A war," said their mother simply.

"A war with—a war with guns and bombs?" asked Cara.

"It may not look like that kind of war. Not at first. But it may become that kind of war, if we don't win quickly enough. It's why we have to fight it. And I'm going to need all of you."

"Then why not Dad?" said Max. "He thinks you left him!"

He shook his head, kicking the ground at his feet.

"Max," said their mother. "Your father is a grown man. He'll be OK. It's you three I'm worried about right now."

"Well, *I'm* worried about him," said Max stubbornly.

"What's happening now dates from long, long before I met your father," she said. "This is a new battle in a very old conflict. And I'm afraid we just can't tell him everything we might like to, Max. There are things going on that are beyond the reaches of what he knows, what he accepts to be the world…"

She paused for a second, then went on.

"Wild happenings," she said.

A chill wind rushed through the pines around them, a sweeping wind that moved the branches roughly for a few moments, dropping needles and cones on the ground, and then settled down again abruptly.

"There are events taking place that would test anyone's threshold. Events that honestly..."

"What?" prompted Cara.

"...that would simply be too much for some people. For their minds to deal with."

"You're saying he couldn't deal? That he'd have some kind of breakdown," said Max flatly.

"The truth is, for all your father's strengths—and they are many—he's not ready for this."

"He's not ready," said Max, "but *we* are?"

"You're different," said their mother. "You're meant to be a part of it. In every life, Max, there's a moment of testing. One moment where things turn. And this is yours. You have to believe, as your sister and brother did. You have to make that leap of faith. They made it already, but you still have to. This is a fight for all of us. And believe me, I wouldn't be doing it if I didn't have to."

"But what are we supposed to say to him?" asked Cara. "Max is right. We're not the only ones who miss you. He's really lonely. This is so *hard* for him, Mom."

"I *know*, sweetheart," said their mother in a voice full of regret. "But you've already seen the danger I put you in, haven't you? You, the people I love most in the world.

You've seen the kind of—elements that are after me. They'd be after him, too, if he knew. Just like they've been after you. And believe it or not, he's actually *more* vulnerable than you are. Because he's not a child anymore, he lacks some of your advantages."

She detached Jax gently from her side and took his hand, then turned and walked over to where a couple of rusting lawn chairs were fallen over. She flipped one upright and sat down on the edge of it, leaning forward. Jax hovered beside her, still clutching her fingers.

"I'm sure," she went on, "that you don't want him exposed to that any more than I do. He doesn't have your resilience, you know. Adults, after all, are more…brittle. In some ways we're harder, and that makes us easier to break."

It occurred to Cara how gracious and elegant she looked, even sitting on a broken chair in her wet hair and bare feet and simple sundress—like a queen.

"You can tell him I spoke to you, if you have to," she said, and sighed. "Tell him I'm—tell him that one day I'll come back. That I want to *now*, but I have a duty. Ask him if he remembers where we first met. Those are my people. Tell him there's a crisis in the world, a crisis that's all around us but whose roots are deeply hidden. But I'm close to those roots, and I have to do what I can. Can you repeat a phrase, Jax?"

"Of course I can, Mom."

"Then tell him this. It's something you already know, something you've seen this week and are beginning to understand, but he doesn't know. Few adults do. It's this: *Die Tiere sind nicht, was sie scheinen.*"

"OK."

"And to you three, I promise: when it's over—when it's really over—then I can come home for good."

"You haven't explained *anything*," said Max. "You're speaking in code."

"The Pouring Man," put in Cara. "He got Rufus killed! I mean, who is he? Really? And why is—was—he after you?"

"He was a servant," said their mother. "A servant of the Cold One, a servant who is not alive. An elemental in the water army. In this war, the enemy has his forces arrayed that way—those who operate through water. Those who operate through earth. Those who use air, those who use fire…and there are others, too. There are other soldiers, other servants. He wasn't unique. But because of your courage, he's gone now. And I'm so…so very sorry about poor old Rufus."

They were silent. Cara felt the push of a little anger at her mother, anger that what she was doing—all of this, even if it wasn't exactly her fault—had hurt Rufus.

Had killed him.

"He was a good dog," said Jax quietly.

For a moment Cara wanted to do nothing but listen to the rhythmic lap of the tide.

"What was that—was that an orca?" she asked finally. "Why are we seeing all these—I mean, orcas and Pacific sea otters and creatures that shouldn't be here? To say nothing of selkies, which aren't even supposed to be real. I mean, why was a sea turtle talking to Jax?"

"Friends," said her mother, and smiled. "Friends have joined the battle. *There are more things in heaven and earth, Horatio, than are dreamt of in your philosophy....*"

"*Hamlet*," said Max, half-grudgingly.

"And those—those pirates? That were ghosts? What was their connection?" pressed Cara.

"They were just captive souls. Some of the souls the Cold One was imprisoning, through one of his servants, so that he could use them. Against us."

"But—I mean, why did it have to be so hard? So—I mean, so mysterious and all that?" asked Cara.

"You had to kept in a state of not knowing until just before we made contact," said their mother. "It's pretty much what Jax intuited: as soon as you knew where I was, *he* would read it in you, and he could get to me. So I had to find a roundabout way of getting to you."

"And what have you—what were you doing all this time?" asked Max.

"I've been hiding from the Cold One and his servants—hiding while I do my work. Where I could safely hide, nearby but unseen. I had to find places where the Cold One couldn't come after me easily—places where *people* couldn't know my whereabouts, you see? So that the Cold One couldn't find me through them. And now that you've taken care of—what did you call him? The Pouring Man?—by making him weak and drawing him to where my friends could come to my defense, I can come out of hiding. Be free. I mean, I can't go to Washington to testify. I can't be that public. But I can at least move around now. I can travel."

"What about the data? Your data set that was stolen?" asked Jax.

"That was him," she said. "His human allies, anyway. I don't know yet *who*, exactly. He has tentacles everywhere. The ocean, you see, is a big part of what we're fighting over...and I've had this—this obligation since before you were born, any of you. It's my—call it a duty to my own family, my own parents and the ones that came before them. I've been running away from it for years. Because I wanted to be here with you and put all of that behind me. But now the scales have tipped, my dears. And I'm needed."

"But your duty is here, too," said Cara desperately. "With us. Isn't it?"

"Of course it is," said their mother. "But you have to remember: I'm doing this for you."

They heard something call out in the night air—a bird, Cara wondered? But it was a loud call, a loud, strange call. There was a grandeur to it, a magnitude.

Their mother rose.

"I have to go," she said. "You bought me some time. But before long there's going to be someone else after me. Just remember: I'm closer than you think. I'm keeping an eye on you. Max, I saw when you broke up that fight in the park...and, of course, I was with you in the car. I had to stop him from hurting you."

Max shook his head.

"How could you be—?"

"And Jax, I was with you at camp. For many days. And I saw you with the leatherback, Ananda. You may need to go to her again."

Jax nodded.

"Cara, I was with you when you climbed onto the roof to push off the skate eggs—which you were right to do, of course. They were his. Not part of him, exactly, but from his world—creatures he sent through water to get to you. Probably he had some other ally bring them up from the sea and drop them there—maybe a gull he turned, I was guessing, since they were on the roof."

"Did you—was that you who talked to me through the otter?"

"You could say that," said her mother.

"But how?"

"I can't answer that for you yet. I will say this: you know how Jax has...some unusual talents?"

She turned and smiled at Jax, hugged him against her side.

"Well. I have some of those, too."

"ESP?" asked Max, the eternal skeptic.

"Something like that...listen. I'll be in touch as soon as I can—or one of our friends will. And I'm sorry you have to be so strong, at your age. Most people don't. But you do. You have to keep your eyes and your minds wide open."

Max still looked, Cara thought, like he was angry.

"Come here, Max," said her mother, and opened her arms.

Max walked to her, but he looked resentful. He was resisting her.

She put her arms around him and whispered something in his ear, something Cara and Jax couldn't hear.

When he pulled back, his face was white, as though he'd had a shock.

And then it resolved.

He nodded and stepped back.

"I have to go, darlings," she said, and turned to Cara.

Cara put her arms around her and hugged her hard. There were tears in her eyes again, she realized, but she wasn't quite as embarrassed as she usually would be.

"At least tell me this one thing—was that you too? With the driftwood?"

"Yes. It was me," whispered her mother.

"Then where were you—where were you hidden?"

"Why, in the sea, of course," whispered her mother. "Now you've freed me. Now I can move through the air, too." And kissed her on the top of her head.

"I love you, Mom," whispered Cara.

"I love you too," said her mother.

"We—we really miss you."

"And I miss you. But it's not forever. Just...till we meet again."

She was walking away through the trees, down toward the water. The three of them followed her, watching.

Something kept them from speaking, kept their eyes glued to her back.

Where are you going, thought Cara. And then, *Who are you* really?

Ahead of their mother was only the water. Cara half expected a ghost ship to sail in and take her away.

Instead something swooped down from the sky—a huge shadow in the dark, a silhouette over the barely visible glitter of the bay. It had a strange, jerky way of flying; she couldn't tell right away what kind of a machine it was. As it drew near, it stirred up the air beneath it so that the reeds bowed low, making a thick, rustling sound that reminded Cara of a helicopter landing. Her mother's hair blew up around her.

It wasn't a machine at all. It was alive.

It alighted somewhere nearby in the trees, which groaned under the massive weight.

"My ride is here," said her mother, and turned to gather them in. Cara didn't want to let go.

"What the hell is *that?*" asked Max, amazed.

"Another friend," said her mother. "Mine and yours too. Our friends are everywhere."

"And our enemies?" asked Cara.

Their mother smiled sadly. "You'll know when I need you. Until then, listen and learn. And remember this before all else: you may sometimes feel alone, but you are not. *You are not alone.*"

"Mom," said Jax suddenly. "Why can't we—why can't I go with you?"

"Not now, Jackson," she said kindly.

Then the enormous, flapping beast descended from the trees onto the reedy mudflats and was hunched over in front of them, its wings stretched out to the sides, its head lowered. Cara couldn't see well anymore—they'd left the headlamps hanging from branches in the backyard—and though she squinted, she couldn't make it out exactly. She couldn't see the head or beak from where she stood, and she thought maybe it wasn't a living thing at all but some kind of an elaborate machine. No bird could possibly be so big.

Her mother stepped onto its back. She took hold of something that almost looked like a pair of reins.

"Stay safe. Remember how much I love you," she said. "Never doubt that."

The dark beast beat its wings and rose up into the sky, their mother standing on it in her bare feet, her hair streaming behind her and the thin sundress flapping. They raised their hands to wave—they couldn't help it, Cara thought, even if the hands would be invisible in the dark.

As the flying thing went up higher, Cara thought she saw her mother sit down, the way you'd ride on a horse, but it all happened too fast for her to be sure.

Soon both of them, their mother and whatever she was riding on, were lost in the dark above—a blot against the field of stars.

And then nothing at all.

The chirping of crickets grew up around them; there was the lapping of the tide. Cara felt the day-to-day world coming back.

She realized she was standing in cool, wet mud and didn't like how it felt; her clothes were clammy and dirty; and the tube of her mother's old lipstick, now warmed by her skin, was still clutched tight in her right hand.

"Jax," said Max, presently. They made their way back up to the house, subdued. "You've gotta know. You always do. All she said was *friend*. But seriously. Talking turtles, mythic women that are half-seal, and now—? What the hell *was* that thing?"

"I can't be sure," said Jax. His voice sounded small. "But it looked an awful lot like a pterosaur."

※

The next morning Cara made toast, put it on a tray with a glass of orange juice, and carried it out to her dad. He'd been working away in his study since before any of them could drag themselves out of bed, but these days he often forgot to eat breakfast.

They had decided she should be the one to talk to him— that she should just say she'd had a conversation with their mother. If Cara said she *alone* had talked to their mother, Max had reasoned, their dad wouldn't feel as singled out.

Also, someone was going to have to tell their dad about Rufus. Say Rufus had run away, or something.... Their dad had loved Rufus. She could barely stand to think about it.

"'Morning, Dad," she said, peeking around the door jamb.

He smiled at her from behind his big desk. He had his chair pushed back, balanced on its two back legs with the front two legs in the air. There was a thick paperback book propped open on his lap, and his sock-clad feet were crossed atop one of the desk's precarious piles of papers, which looked like the Leaning Tower of Pisa.

"Good morning," he said.

She pushed the door open with her elbow, since she had the breakfast tray in her hands. The curtains had been pulled wide open and light streamed in from the sky; she could see the high, clear blue, the fleecy clouds, and the sparkle of the water out the window behind him. The room seemed kind of golden, and her dad actually looked all right—better than he had the day before, jammed miserably into the red sports car with not enough room for his guilt over Max.

"I made you some toast," she said. "With the butter all melted and lots of raspberry jam. Your favorite, right?"

"Very thoughtful of you, my dear," he said, and smiled at her.

She went up to the desk and set the plate down.

"I can make you coffee, too, if you want," she added.

"Well, this is the VIP treatment," he said. "What did I do to deserve it?"

"Listen," she said, and perched opposite him on the arm of one of the big chairs. "It's a kind of small celebration."

"Oh? What are we celebrating, then?" He picked up a piece of toast, biting in.

"Dad. Do you trust me?"

"Of course I do," he said, chewing.

"You know how, back in the early part of the summer, from time to time—even though she never picked up—I would, you know, try Mom's cell," she said. It was true. "Remember?"

"I do. Jax and Max, too. And eventually we decided you kids should stop it, that it was getting you down. Hearing her talk on the voice mail and never reaching her."

"But so, I tried again, just, kind of, for something to do. You know, like randomly, because I was bummed out or whatever. Yesterday night."

"Mmm," said her dad, and nodded slowly, cocking his head to one side to keep listening. She thought he was trying not to look judgmental.

"And the thing is…" A white lie, she thought. For his own good. "She picked up."

Her dad stopped mid-chew, slowly setting his half-eaten toast down on the desk. Lifting his feet carefully off his desk, setting them on the floor, and sitting forward. The front legs of the chair made a cracking sound as they hit the floor. As though in a daze, he brushed his hands together, maybe to clear them of a fine dusting of crumbs.

"She picked up," he repeated, dully.

"She really misses you," Cara put in quickly.

He was staring down at his hands, spaced out, now, on the desk in front of him as though bracing him against it.

"Cara," he said. "This isn't something to kid about."

"Dad. Look at me," she said. She realized she was twisting her good-luck ring, the nazar. "Do I look like I'm joking? I wouldn't do that to you. Or myself, either. I'm not making it up. I'm not inventing or joking or fantasizing or anything like that. *I talked to her*. You need to believe me."

He nodded slowly, gazing at her face. She saw how isolated he felt—as though the ground, all of a sudden, wasn't so steady beneath him. And then he faded from view and she saw something more—two children, walking along the seacliffs together, where the wild roses grew. Their clothes were kind of retro—it had happened long ago, she knew. In the seventies, maybe. Then she recognized them: her parents. Their faces were so young. No lines on them or anything, clear skin and bright, perfect eyes.

They stopped at the edge of the cliff and looked out at the ocean together, smiling and holding hands.

"I know she promised once, on the cliffs, that she would never leave you," she said softly as her dad came back into focus.

That was what they'd been saying, though she'd seen it rather than heard their words. It was almost shocking to see him again the way he looked now—old and complicated. And far more resigned than he'd looked then. Kids' faces, she realized, had so much less *in* them than adult ones. Sure they were beautiful, but they were kind of blank, too.

It was the first time she'd seen something in the course of normal life, she realized. The first time a vision had come to her where it felt like her own.

"This was beyond her control," she went on. "She can't be in touch with you because it's too dangerous for her here. There are people looking for her. People she doesn't want to bring near...near us. She said it was her old life catching up with her, people she knew from way back. And she said to give you a message. Maybe so you know it was really her I talked to?"

Her dad raised his hands, spread open as though asking for something. He was the motion of his hands, she thought. Their gestures spoke for him when he couldn't.

"She said, if you remember where you met? That those were her people, I think was what she said. And she's been caught up in this—situation with them, this crisis.... She said something like: *Tell him I have an obligation older than anything he knows.* Something like that. It's at the root of everything that's going on, she said...."

As she told him the rest of the message, he listened without moving. His eyes were focused sharply on her, as though he was concentrating on remembering every word.

"And one more thing," she finished. "It's in another language. Dutch or—or Scandinavian or something? I just know how it's pronounced. *Die Tiere sind night, was sie scheinen.*"

He picked up a pen and wrote something down.

"So, but, the thing is," she finished lamely. "She's alive. She's OK. And she said to say, most of all...she, you know. She loves you. And all that."

Her dad stopped writing. And then, without meeting her eyes, he turned around slowly, turned and stared out his big bay window toward the ocean.

"I'm sorry," whispered Cara.

She waited. Her dad, his back still turned, gazing through the window with the light of late morning streaming past him, seemed grief-stricken. Dust motes swirled in the sunbeams, reminding her of the red tide...air and water, the world somehow the same in all its mediums...she stared at them. Maybe he didn't believe any of it. After all, it wasn't really what had happened....

But then he turned back around to face her. He was smiling slightly, but he also had something else in his face, something hard.

He wasn't letting their mother off the hook, she thought. Not right now, anyway.

"Thank you for telling me, sweetheart," he said. "I'd rather she'd spoken to me herself, of course. But thank you."

He ran a hand through his hair.

"She—I know she *wanted* to," said Cara.

"It's not your responsibility," he said. "You've done well. You've done just what you should, coming to me. So please, don't worry."

"There's something else," said Cara, nervous. "It's—it's something not good. Rufus is gone. He—he's not in the house. We don't know where he is."

(Technically, that wasn't a lie. Because who knew where the orca was now?)

"Well. All right, honey. We'll take a walk around the neighborhood and look for him."

He didn't know it was serious yet, but that was OK. They could look for Rufus. They could go through the motions, for their dad.

They wouldn't find him, of course.

Rufus had been twelve—a grandfather, in Labrador years. Maybe her father would come to believe he'd slunk off into a private place to die, as old dogs sometimes did.

"And we'll get that pizza tonight, all right? We'll rent an old movie. We'll talk about starting back to school. Sound good?"

She nodded.

The walk to "look" for Rufus was worse than she'd expected. All four of them started out together along their street, away from the water, calling and whistling. That part was bad. Cara felt like a liar, felt bad they had to do the charade for their dad's benefit. It seemed wrong, and somehow disrespectful of Roof. She still felt so guilty; Max and Jax had both said it wasn't their fault, and her mother had said so, too, but it didn't really matter what anyone said. There had to have been a way of saving him. And she hadn't seen it. And now he was gone, and he didn't deserve to be.

For a while she thought about begging off—saying she felt sick suddenly and could the others keep looking without her?—but then she caught Max's eye and realized he felt as miserable as she did.

And a couple of minutes later, Hayley's car passed them and then slowed down and stopped, pulled over against the curb.

"Well hey there, Sykeses!" called her mom cheerily, rolling down the driver's-side window. "Whatcha doing?"

They clustered around the car, Cara bending down to wave to Hayley in the passenger seat as her dad explained to Hayley's mother that they were looking for Rufus. Cara walked around the car as Hayley rolled down her own window.

"So—what happened? Did it work?" asked Hayley, low.

"It worked," whispered Cara. "We *saw her.*"

"OMG," breathed Hayley. "No way!"

"Shh!"

"And so—?"

"I'll tell you about on the cell later, OK?"

"Why don't you all come over for dinner?" asked her mom. "I have this new recipe I'd love to try out on you! Do you like prawns, William?"

Looking at Hayley's mom smiling up at her dad from behind the steering wheel—with her frosted hair and shiny lipstick and tanned cleavage showing—it occurred to Cara for the first time: she *liked* him.

Hayley's mom had a *crush* on her dad. Seriously.

Ew. She tried to wipe the thought away.

Hopefully she was wrong.

"Sure," her dad was saying when she paid attention again. "Sure, that sounds great."

He wouldn't like her, anyway. She wasn't his type at all. For one thing, she wore press-on nails.

"Maybe we should split up," suggested Jax, after Hayley's car pulled away again. "Go looking separately. Cover more ground."

"OK," said their dad. "Max can come with me; Cara and Jax, why don't you circle around over there." And he pointed.

After that the fake search was more bearable, since she and Jax didn't have to pretend. They just walked along in a glum but companionable silence, remembering their dog.

⚎

"Die Tiere sind nicht, was sie scheinen," said Jax softly.

It was later, in Cara's room. Their dad had given up on looking for Rufus, for now; he was puzzled, but he said they should put a bowl of food out on the porch and maybe Rufus would come back. Max had gone out to help Zee get the scuba gear back from where Jax and Cara had left it, hidden in the scrubby vegetation atop the bluffs. He had to do it right away, before her father found out the gear was missing and she got in serious trouble.

The afternoon was warm, and someone in the neighborhood was having a barbecue again, Cara guessed: the smell of woodsy smoke drifted in her open window. She could hear the tinkly music of an ice-cream truck down the street.

"What?"

"Thing is, I could see it. I could read the letters in her mind, though I can't read all of Mom. She's a hard one to read. There are things in there that are hidden to me...."

"Jax," broke in Cara. "Did you really want—did you want to go with her?"

"Maybe," said Jax. "Didn't you?"

"I don't know," said Cara. "I want her to come back here, is what *I* want."

Jax nodded slowly.

"You wouldn't have left me, though, would you?" she asked.

"I won't leave you," said Jax solemnly.

Their eyes met. Cara smiled, and then Jax did, too.

"Anyway," he picked up again. "I did see the sentence. I read it. So I didn't need to just go by the sounds; I knew how it was written."

"And?" she asked.

"It turns out to be German," he said.

"So what does it mean?"

"I translated it online," he said, and handed her a scrap of paper. "It took all of five seconds. If Mom wanted to keep the message secret from us, she should have remembered we have access to basic software technology. Of course, she's right in that *we* already know the substance of the message—in one sense, at least. Where

247

maybe Dad doesn't. But whatever. I wrote it down for you."

She looked down at the big, block letters of his kid's handwriting.

THE ANIMALS ARE NOT WHAT THEY SEEM.

Lydia Millet is the author of many novels for adult readers, including *My Happy Life,* which won the PEN-USA Award for Fiction in 2003, and *Oh Pure and Radiant Heart,* about the scientists who designed the first atomic bomb, which was shortlisted for the UK's Arthur C. Clarke Prize. Her story collection *Love in Infant Monkeys* was a finalist for the 2010 Pulitzer Prize. She has taught at Columbia University and the University of Arizona and now works as a writer and editor at an endangered-species protection group. This is her first novel for young readers.

She is working on the second book in the Dissenters series, The Shimmers in the Night.